# ▶▶▶ACCEL·WORLD

## PULL OF THE DARK NEBULA

**REKI KAWAHARA**

ILLUSTRATION BY
**HIMA**

DESIGN BY
**bee-pee**

MW00834675

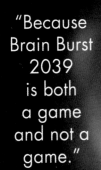

"Because Brain Burst 2039 is both a game and not a game."

"Silver Crow. Your impression that the settings of this game are contradictory is entirely correct."

## TRILEAD TETROXIDE

Avatar Haruyuki met when he entered the Castle. Trilead is a pseudonym; his real avatar name is Azure Air.

## GRAPHITE EDGE

One of the Four Elements and an executive of the former Nega Nebulus. His objective and true identity is, as always, shrouded in mystery.

"That is the final Arc, the Fluctuating Light..."

"From here, you can't tell what kind of item it is."

"The battle power of the Eight Divines that guard it exceeds even that of the Four Gods."

## SILVER CROW

Member of the new Nega Nebulus. Possesses the sole flying ability in the Accelerated World. Real world: Haruyuki Arita.

## SKY RAKER

Member of the new Nega Nebulus. Incarnate Master who taught Haruyuki. Real world: Fuko Kurasaki.

"Wh-what manner of behavior is this, servant?! Do you consider this sort of insolent action to be appropriate for a servant?!"

## METATRON

True form of the archangel that lives in the deepest level of Shiba Park Underground Labyrinth, one of the four major dungeons in the Accelerated World. Treats Silver Crow like her servant.

**SATOMI MITO**
Duel avatar:
Mint Mitten.

**SHIHOKO NAGO**
Duel avatar:
Chocolat Puppeter.

**YUME YURUKI**
Duel avatar:
Plum Flipper.

**? ? ?**

**UTAI SHINOMIYA**
Duel avatar:
Ardor Maiden.

**KUROYUKIHIME**
Duel avatar:
Black Lotus.

**FUKO KURASAKI**
Duel avatar:
Sky Raker.

**RIN KUSAKABE**
Duel avatar:
Ash Roller.

**CHIYURI KURASHIMA**
Duel avatar: Lime Bell.

**AKIRA HIMI**
Duel avatar:
Aqua Current.

## Legions of Pure Color

### Black Legion: Nega Nebulus
Master: Black Lotus (Kuroyukihime)
Executive branch name: Four Elements
Wind: Sky Raker (Fuko Kurasaki)
Fire: Ardor Maiden (Utai Shinomiya)
Water: Aqua Current (Akira Himi)
Lime Bell (Chiyuri Kurashima)
Cyan Pile (Takumu Mayuzumi)
Silver Crow (Haruyuki Arita)

### Red Legion: Prominence
Master: Scarlet Rain (Yuniko Kozuki)
Executive branch name: Triplex
No. 1: Blood Leopard (Mihaya Kakei)
No. 2: Cassis Moose
No. 3: Thistle Porcupine
Blaze Heart
Peach Parasol
Ochre Prison
Mustard Salticid

### Blue Legion: Leonids
Master: Blue Knight
Executive branch name: Dualis
Cobalt Blade (Koto Takanouchi)
Manganese Blade (Yuki Takanouchi)
Frost Horn
Tourmaline Shell

### Green Legion: Great Wall
Master: Green Grandé
Executive branch name: Six Armors
First seat: Graphite Edge
Second seat: Viridian Decurion
Third seat: Iron Pound
Fourth seat: Lignum Vitae
Fifth seat: Suntan Chafer
Sixth seat: ???
Ash Roller (Rin Kusakabe)
Bush Utan
Olive Grab
Jade Jailer

### Yellow Legion: Crypt Cosmic Circus
Master: Yellow Radio
Lemon Pierette
Sax Loader

### Purple Legion: Aurora Oval
Master: Purple Thorn
Executive branch name: ???
Aster Vine

### White Legion: Oscillatory Universe
Master: White Cosmos
Executive branch name: Seven Dwarves
Ivory Tower

## Other Legions

Acceleration Research Society
Black Vise
Argon Array
Dusk Taker (Seiji Nomi)
Rust Jigsaw
Sulfur Pot
Wolfram Cerberus (Armor of Catastrophe Mark II)

### Petit Paquet
Master: Chocolat Puppeter (Shihoko Nago)
Mint Mitten (Satomi Mito)
Plum Flipper (Yume Yuruki)

### Computation and Martial Arts Research Club
Aluminum Valkyrie (Chiaki Chigira)
Orange Raptor (Yuko Hori)
Violet Dancer (Kurumi Kuruma)
Iris Alice (Lilya Usachova)

### Affiliation unknown
Magenta Scissor (Rui Odagiri)
Avocado Avoider
Trilead Tetroxide
Nickel Doll
Sand Duct
Crimson Kingbolt
Lagoon Dolphin (Ruka Asato)
Coral Merrow (Mana Itosu)
Orchid Oracle
Tin Writer

## Enemies

### Four Divines
Archangel Metatron (Shiba Park underground labyrinth)
Goddess Nyx (Yoyogi Park underground labyrinth)
???
???

### Four Gods of the Four Gates
East gate: Seiryu
West gate: Byakko
South gate: Suzaku
North gate: Genbu
Eight Gods of the Shrine of the Eight Divines
???

Duel avatar and Enemy list

# ▶▶▶ *ACCEL · WORLD* 19

## PULL OF THE DARK NEBULA

Reki Kawahara
Illustrations: HIMA
Design: bee-pee

YEN
ON

NEW YORK

■ Kuroyukihime = Umesato Junior High School student council vice president. Trim and clever girl who has it all. Her background is shrouded in mystery. Her in-school avatar is a spangle butterfly she programmed herself. Her duel avatar is the Black King, Black Lotus (level nine).

■ Haruyuki = Haruyuki Arita. Eighth grader at Umesato Junior High School. Bullied, on the pudgy side. He's good at games, but shy. His in-school avatar is a pink pig. His duel avatar is Silver Crow (level five).

■ Chiyuri = Chiyuri Kurashima. Haruyuki's childhood friend. Meddling, energetic girl. Her in-school avatar is a silver cat. Her duel avatar is Lime Bell (level four).

■ Takumu = Takumu Mayuzumi. A boy Haruyuki and Chiyuri have known since childhood. Good at kendo. His duel avatar is Cyan Pile (level five).

■ Fuko = Fuko Kurasaki. Burst Linker belonging to the old Nega Nebulus. One of the Four Elements. Rules wind. Lived as a recluse due to certain circumstances but was persuaded by Kuroyukihime and Haruyuki to come back to the battlefront. Taught Haruyuki about the Incarnate System. Her duel avatar is Sky Raker (level eight).

■ Uiui = Utai Shinomiya. Burst Linker belonging to the old Nega Nebulus. One of the Four Elements. Rules fire. Fourth grader in the elementary division of Matsunogi Academy. Not only can she use the advanced curse removal command "Purify," she is also skilled at long-range attacks. Her duel avatar is Ardor Maiden (level seven).

■ Current = Formally known as Aqua Current. Real name: Akira Himi. Burst Linker belonging to the old Nega Nebulus. One of the Four Elements. Rules water. Known as "The One," the bouncer who undertakes the protection of new Burst Linkers.

■ Graphite Edge = Real name: unknown. Burst Linker belonging to the old Nega Nebulus. One of the Four Elements. Their identity is still wrapped in mystery.

---

■ Neurolinker = A portable Internet terminal that connects with the brain via a wireless quantum connection and enhances all five senses with images, sounds, and other stimuli.

■ Brain Burst = Neurolinker application sent to Haruyuki by Kuroyukihime.

■ Duel avatar = Player's virtual self, operated when fighting in Brain Burst.

■ Legion = Groups composed of many duel avatars with the objective of expanding occupied areas and securing rights. There are seven main Legions, each led by one of the Seven Kings of Pure Color.

■ Normal Duel Field = The field where normal Brain Burst battles (one-on-one) are carried out. Although the specs do possess elements of reality, the system is essentially on the level of an old-school fighting game.

■ Unlimited Neutral Field = Field for high-level players where only duel avatars at levels four and up are allowed. The game system is of a wholly different order than that of the Normal Duel Field, and the level of freedom in this field beats out even the next-generation VRMMO.

---

■ Movement Control System = System in charge of avatar control. Normally, this system handles all avatar movement.

■ Image Control System = System in which the player creates a strong image in their mind to operate the avatar. The mechanism is very different from the normal Movement Control System, and very few players can use it. Key component of the Incarnate System.

■ Incarnate System = Technique allowing players to interfere with the Brain Burst program's Image Control System to bring about a reality outside of the game's framework. Also referred to as "overwriting" game phenomena.

---

■ Acceleration Research Society = Mysterious Burst Linker group. They do not think of Brain Burst as a simple fighting game and are planning something. Black Vise and Rust Jigsaw are members.

■ Armor of Catastrophe = An Enhanced Armament also called "Chrome Disaster." Equipped with this, an avatar can use powerful abilities such as Drain, which absorbs the HP of the enemy avatar, and Divination, which calculates enemy attacks in advance to evade them. However, the spirit of the wearer is polluted by Chrome Disaster, which comes to rule the wearer completely.

■ Star Caster = The longsword carried by Chrome Disaster. Although it now has a sinister form, it was originally a famous and solemn sword that shone like a star, just as the name suggests.

■ ISS kit = Abbreviation for "IS mode study kit." ("IS mode" is "Incarnate System mode.") The kit allows any duel avatar who uses it to make use of the Incarnate System. While using it, a red "eye" is attached to some part of the avatar, and a black aura overlay—the staple of Incarnate attacks— is emitted from the eye.

■ Seven Arcs = The seven strongest Enhanced Armaments in the Accelerated World. They are the greatsword Impulse, the staff Tempest, the large shield Strife, the Luminary (form unknown), the straight sword Infinity, the full-body armor Destiny, and the Fluctuating Light (form unknown).

■ Mental-Scar Shell = The emotional scars that are the foundation of a duel avatar (mental scars created from trauma in early childhood)—this is the shell enveloping them. Children with exceptionally hard and thick "shells" are said to produce metal-color duel avatars.

■ Artificial metal color = Refers to a metal-color avatar that is not generated naturally from the subject's mental scars, but rather produced artificially by a third party through the thickening of the Mental-Scar Shell.

■ Unlimited EK = Abbreviation for Unlimited Enemy Kill. The subject avatar is killed by a powerful Enemy in the Unlimited Neutral Field, and each time they regenerate (after a fixed period of time), they are killed again by that Enemy, falling into an infinite hell.

▶▶▶*ACCEL·WORLD*

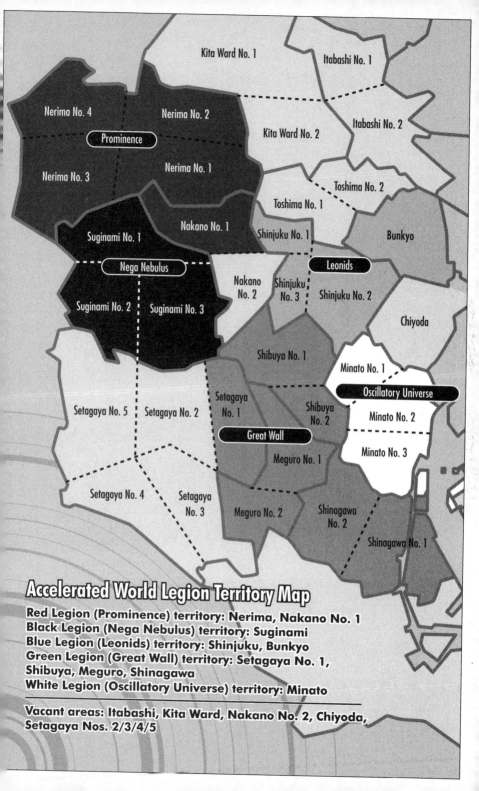

Kita Ward No. 1

Itabashi No. 1

Nerima No. 4

Nerima No. 2

Itabashi No. 2

Prominence

Kita Ward No. 2

Nerima No. 3

Nerima No. 1

Toshima No. 2

Toshima No. 1

Suginami No. 1

Nakano No. 1

Shinjuku No. 1

Bunkyo

Nega Nebulus

Leonids

Nakano No. 2

Shinjuku No. 3

Shinjuku No. 2

Suginami No. 2

Suginami No. 3

Chiyoda

Shibuya No. 1

Minato No. 1

Setagaya No. 5

Setagaya No. 2

Setagaya No. 1

Oscillatory Universe

Minato No. 2

Shibuya No. 2

Great Wall

Meguro No. 1

Minato No. 3

Setagaya No. 4

Setagaya No. 3

Meguro No. 2

Shinagawa No. 2

Shinagawa No. 1

# Accelerated World Legion Territory Map

**Red Legion (Prominence) territory:** Nerima, Nakano No. 1
**Black Legion (Nega Nebulus) territory:** Suginami
**Blue Legion (Leonids) territory:** Shinjuku, Bunkyo
**Green Legion (Great Wall) territory:** Setagaya No. 1,
Shibuya, Meguro, Shinagawa
**White Legion (Oscillatory Universe) territory:** Minato

**Vacant areas:** Itabashi, Kita Ward, Nakano No. 2, Chiyoda,
Setagaya Nos. 2/3/4/5

# 1

There was only one way to become a Burst Linker, a player of the fighting game Brain Burst 2039: get a current Burst Linker to copy and install the BB program.

To do this, the would-be Burst Linker needed a wired connection with the current Burst Linker's Neurolinker. If the installation succeeded, giver and receiver would be bound by the transitory and yet most powerful bond in the Accelerated World: that of "parent" and "child."

Haruyuki's parent was Black Lotus, the Black King, aka Kuroyukihime. Utai Shinomiya's parent was Mirror Masker, aka her real-life older brother, Kyoya Shinomiya. Rin Kusakabe's parent was Akira, aka Fuko Kurasaki. And Fuko's parent was...

*Now that I'm thinking about it, I've never heard Master Raker talk about her parent*, Haruyuki thought as he glanced over at her, but he hurriedly pulled his mind back from that potential tangent to focus on the current situation.

Thursday, July 18, 2047. 5:00 PM.

Together with Fuko, Haruyuki had dived into the Unlimited Neutral Field from the Arita living room, charged the Castle with the borrowed power of the Archangel Metatron, and entered the fortress for the first time in about a month and a half of real-world time. There, he'd been reunited with his friend Trilead Tetroxide and one other person: the Anomaly Graphite Edge, first seat of the Six Armors, the Green Legion, Great Wall, executive.

Trilead introduced Graph to Haruyuki and Fuko as his swordmaster and Brain Burst parent. In other words, Graph was the one who had given the mysterious young warrior Trilead the program. And to carry out the required copy/install, they had to have had a direct connection between their Neurolinkers in the real world.

"...Trilead...And Graph...," Haruyuki said to the pair lined up before him, still in shock. "You're...You know each other in the real?"

Trilead looked up at Graph with a slight frown, and Graph shrugged lightly.

"Mm, we'll explain that a bit later, Crow," he said. "Rekka's looks like she's got some questions for us, first."

"Huh?" As Haruyuki shifted his gaze back to Sky Raker, his avatar reflexively stiffened up.

Her madder-red eye lenses shone with a particular light, quiet but hiding an unfathomable force, and that was all he needed to see to understand that the "actually scary Master Raker" was one step away from intense rage.

"Graphite Edge."

She called him by his full avatar name, and Graph shuffled backward ever so slightly.

"Wh-what's up, Rekka?"

"The fact that you are here in this place...I take it to mean that you long ago escaped from the Unlimited EK the God Genbu had you in at the north gate of the Castle?"

"W-well, strictly speaking, I guess so?"

"And when, exactly, did this happen?"

"A-actually, pretty soon after the Castle attack three years ago..."

"So then...why did you not tell us sooner?!" she shouted, pale-blue flames of a powerful aura jetting up around her slender avatar.

Haruyuki once again flinched into himself. Even Metatron's icon, which had apparently been observing their surroundings from her spot on his right shoulder, froze in place.

"Do you have *any* idea how much it has pained Maiden that you were trapped in an Unlimited EK?! In order to save you, that child has gone so far as to train in an Incarnate technique of the fourth quadrant—large-scale destruction!! Her! With her kind heart; kinder than anyone else's!!"

This was true. During their previous Castle escape mission, Ardor Maiden—Utai Shinomiya—had activated a fearsome Incarnate technique that changed the ground to magma in order to dispatch large soldier Enemies. He was pretty sure she said at the time that she developed the technique for the God Genbu.

The more the practitioner used fourth quadrant—negative Incarnate techniques—the more they were pulled into the hole in their heart. Specifically, they felt more and more negative emotions toward themselves and other people, leading to a warping of their personality. All that awaited any player captured by the darkness in the depths of that hole was a dark carnage, the simple and singular search for enemies and constant battle until the player was utterly destroyed. Just like had happened to Chrome Falcon, after becoming the first Chrome Disaster.

*Which reminds me. It was here in the Castle where Falcon's Enhanced Armament, The Destiny, was found...*

His thoughts now started to wander into the past, but his mind was yanked back by Graph's voice and the ever-so-slightly serious edge it now held.

"She was...Denden...Ah, crap, I didn't mean to..." Scratching his helmet with one hand, the dual swordmaster raised the other and continued, half in apology, half in excuse, "It's true, it's on me for not telling Lota and the rest of you that I escaped from Genbu's Unlimited EK. But, y'know, how was I supposed to let you know? I don't have your e-mail addresses or anything. And just showing up all of a sudden to pick a fight in a duel's a whole thing..."

"You didn't have to come meet face-to-face. There are all kinds of ways to send a message!" Fuko thundered, and Haruyuki flinched along with Graph. "Great Wall often attacks Suginami in the Territories, so you could have had that team give us a message. Or you could have simply failed in some spectacular manner in the Unlimited Neutral Field like you used to do in the old days. If we heard you'd shown up and blundered in some ridiculous way, we'd at least know you escaped from the Unlimited EK."

"Y-you're totally right. But the second one o' those is kinda impossible."

"And why's that?" Fuko pressed.

"I *did* make it out of the Unlimited EK," Graph replied, not hesitant in the least. "But not outside the Castle. I escaped to the inside."

"…The inside?"

"Yep. I know I'm pretty amazing, but there's no way I could dodge Genbu's attacks and make it across the bridge on my own. But my appearance point was right next to the north gate, so I figured I might have a chance that way. Like, 'why not give it a try?' And that means when I'm in the Unlimited Neutral Field, I'm here inside the Castle."

"B-but that doesn't make any sense!" Haruyuki cried out heedlessly.

The swordsman's face mask was abruptly whirled around toward him. He definitely wasn't threatening Haruyuki, but the instant the sharp lines of his goggles were turned his way, Haruyuki felt an impact from the completely natural posture—something unfathomable—and his breath stopped.

"Um." Slowly exhaling the virtual air trapped in his lungs, Haruyuki first checked one thing. "Graph, three years ago… You came into the Castle after the first Nega Nebulus mission to attack it, which is where you met Trilead and made him your child, right?"

Dual swordmaster and apprentice nodded firmly at the same time, so he continued.

"To get into the Castle through one of the four gates without defeating the Four Gods, the seal plate on the inside of the gate has to be destroyed in advance. Like Trilead did for us. But when you charged the gate, Graph, Trilead wasn't a Burst Linker yet, so there was no one inside who could destroy the plate— No, I guess you could make Trilead your child first and then get him to cut the seal? But then, how did *you* get inside, Trilead…?" The whole thing gradually made less and less sense to him, and he trailed off as he looked back and forth at the two of them.

Again, Trilead said nothing, but rather glanced at his teacher with a faint hint of a smile. Graph, on the other hand, groaned before turning his face to the massive building rising up behind them.

"How about we go somewhere we can relax at least? The patrol Enemies'll be regenerating pretty soon."

"I agree." This immediate response came not from Fuko or Haruyuki, but Metatron's icon on Haruyuki's shoulder. "This palace—you little warriors call it the Castle, yes? I wish to see the interior right away. Postpone the information exchange and move there immediately."

"You're somehow even more domineering now, hmm?" Fuko murmured, shaking her head in exasperation, her anger finally subsiding.

When Haruyuki and Utai had broken into the Castle a month ago, the field attribute had been a Heian stage, and a Demon City stage when they'd escaped. Now, on his third visit to this court-yard, it was a Moonlight stage, but only the object design had been transformed; the terrain itself was unchanged. The wide, straight road from the plaza in front of the Castle's south gate stretched out to the north, and up ahead, the main building sat ponderous, now a massive temple.

The last time, fearsome Enemies had been patrolling the corridors when he'd headed for the main building with Utai, so they'd had to use the lines of pillars to either side and carefully jump from the protective cover of one to the next, which ate up a lot of his mental energy. But now, Graph and Trilead had dispatched those guard Enemies, so they could walk tall down the center of the road that was likely patterned after the Suzaku Avenue of the ancient capital.

And while this was utterly ideal, and he was quite grateful for it, it also made the questions in his mind multiply. He looked at Graph and Lead walking slightly ahead of him and wondered how on earth they had known that Haruyuki and Fuko would try breaking into the Castle that particular day at that particular time. He'd only told Fuko what he was planning, and then only fifteen or so minutes before the start of the mission. He was sure she hadn't had time to contact anyone else either, and she had no reason to. Given her earlier anger, it was obvious that she hadn't expected to see Graph here again.

So then, had they anticipated Haruyuki's move and been waiting for him? He was aware that he was pretty easy to read, so he couldn't say it was entirely unexpected that someone would guess what he was up to. But even so, it wasn't realistic to wait for someone in the Unlimited Neutral Field. Time here flowed a thousand times faster. No matter how patient the Burst Linker, six months was basically as long as anyone could keep waiting for someone who might not even show up. Even the Green King, Green Grandé, and the third seat of the Six Armors, Iron Pound, were going to give up their stakeout at three months when they tried to wait for the Change to effect a Hell stage so they would have a chance of defeating the Metatron who'd been guarding Tokyo Midtown Tower.

*Well, G by himself could probably hold out for a whole year, though...*

As this thought passed through his mind, he shook his head vigorously. Haruyuki would never be able to sit tight for a whole year. He had no doubt that the master and student before him were equipped with far more patience than he was, but he still found it hard to believe they would wait blindly and possibly in vain. Most likely, they had guessed at Haruyuki and Fuko's plan through some means or another—and with a fair bit of precision...

"This is such a lovely place."

A voice came suddenly from his left, and Haruyuki shifted his gaze.

Having dismissed the Gale Thruster, Fuko was once again wearing her white hat and dress, and she looked at their surroundings, seemingly moved. He heard a faint murmur come from her face mask with its molding surprisingly similar to her real-world face.

"This mission is for Sacchi, but still, it's honestly a shame that she's not here. She's the one more than anyone in this world... who wants to know the truth of the Accelerated World..."

"Yeah." Haruyuki nodded, reflecting upon that same thought. Silver Crow and Sky Raker, with their flight abilities, had only barely made it through the area guarded by the God Suzaku and had used up every bit of power and energy they had to do it—they'd definitely had no margin for bringing a third person. Still, if they could have brought Kuroyukihime, she would no doubt have been utterly delighted. He remembered how her eyes had shone as she listened to him and Utai alternately explain the situation inside the Castle and hung his head.

"I do not understand." A crisp voice came from his right shoulder. "Why are you little ones held prisoner by thoughts of what you cannot do, allowing your thoughts to stagnate? It is quite unproductive. If you have the time for that, think about what you can do going forward and activate your mental circuits. Unfortunately, there are no words to express this situation precisely in my word library."

The Archangel Metatron spoke 1.2 times faster than normal, and he flashed a secret smile that was overwritten by a feeling of admiration. She was right—and while he didn't necessarily agree that reviewing the past was pointless, right now, it was more important that they turn their eyes to the future.

"We call this status 'excitement,'" he said, turning his face to his shoulder.

The 3-D icon blinked irregularly for a moment. "I shall remember that. Now then, I order you anew. Crow. And Raker. You must be at full excitement in this situation."

"I never dreamed the day would come when an Enemy told me to be excited," Fuko murmured.

"You will say *Being*," came the quick rejoinder. But Metatron quickly rattled on, "Currently, we are in Area Zero Zero, the place where Brain Burst 2039 begins and ends. Even a single terrain object is utterly fascinating! Have you realized this? With the current field attribution HL05—what you little warriors call the Moonlight stage, the object endurance should be less than average, and yet, everything here is set at the maximum value. And all main architectural object structures have the attribute 'indestructible'...My own Trisagion most likely would not be able to cause their destruction."

"...You really *are* excited, sounding so happy about things you can't do," Haruyuki noted.

"I feel as though that utterance was relatively insolent, but I shall allow it. Now, look behind us. It appears the guard Beings are regenerating."

"You keep telling me to look at things; I can't keep up here..." He turned, sending sparks scattering on the paving stones, and immediately shouted, "Wheah?!"

In the plaza in front of the south gate, a mere fifty meters away, he could see a large-scale cascade effect.

"Hmm, that's quite the information density. As with the guard Beings in use at the headquarters of the Acceleration Research Society, it will be difficult to repel it with my order."

"That's too bad—Now's not the time for that kind of talk!" Whirling around once again, he called out to Graphite Edge ahead. "Uh! Um! Graph! It looks like the Beings—I mean, Enemies—are generating!"

The swordsman glanced over his shoulder at the eerie gushing effect before answering lackadaisically, "It's fine; we're fine. They're not gonna aggro when we're this far away."

"B-but it's not like Enemies just stay in one fixed place, though, right…?"

"It's fine; we're fine. Those guys are slow."

"B-but it's not going to be just that one, though, right…?"

"It's fine; we're fine— Oh! We're not fine."

At Graph's latest reaction, Haruyuki timidly looked back to find a second cascade had started a scant ten meters away. A distance at which they would certainly be attacked if discovered.

"S-seeeeee?!"

"Welp! Everybody run!"

The swordmaster took off toward the main building so fast that he left a gray afterimage hanging in the air.

"Heeeeeeeey!"

*So irresponsible!* Haruyuki cursed as he hurried to chase after him.

"I'm sorry, Crow." Lead, running next to him, bowed his head apologetically. "My master is always like that."

"N-no, you don't have to apologize, Lead…"

"When a person's with *that* boy," Fuko said darkly from behind, "everything is like this, so you'd best get used to it sooner rather than later, Corvus."


After a minute or two of dashing, Haruyuki made it to the plaza in front of the main building in one piece and let out a long breath.

Graphite Edge was already there, hand up to shield his eyes, staring in the direction of the south gate. "Aah, they're just re-popping like bunnies out there. Gonna have to clear them away again…Hey, Crow, Rekka, you have to help when you leave."

"What…?" Haruyuki stiffened in place. *Defeat that entire Enemy squad?!*

"If you did it once, you can do it again, Graph," Fuko responded.

"Aah, that hurts." Graphite Edge winced. "You got any idea how hard Lead and I worked to clear them away for you?"

"Yes, yes. And you'll have our thanks for that. In our deepest heart of hearts," she finished, effectively silencing Graph.

It was Lead who spoke next, instead. "The Enemies guarding the main entrance of the main building will be recovered soon. Let's go inside before they are."

Haruyuki's memories of his previous visit came back to him now. The design of the main building was significantly different here in the Moonlight stage than it had been in the Heian stage before, but the basic structure and Enemy placement would have been the same. And the last time, the two terrifying Enemies had stood on either side of the main entrance, blocking the way, clearly on a different scale from the other guards.

"D-did you actually defeat those two monsters?!" Haruyuki asked, stunned.

"Yes." Lead nodded bashfully. "Although I was merely assisting my master."

"No...Just the fact that you fought them is plenty amazing." Haruyuki looked once more at the young blue warrior before him. He felt like he had grown a little at least over the last month, and it seemed like Lead was also not the same person Haruyuki had first met.

*I want to hurry up and get somewhere safe so we can talk more.* Suppressing his impatience, Haruyuki climbed the large stairs with the rest of the group.

The main entrance was a set of imposing, metal double doors, apparently in the Western design of the Moonlight stage. In terms of size, at least, they didn't compare with the massive doors of the four gates, but they were as splendid as he'd expect from a building that sat in the center of this world, the pale moonlight reflecting off the complicated geometrical designs on the surface.

"Now, Crow. Here we have the fifth of the ninefold gate, the central door. Please go ahead and open it." Lead urged him forward with a wave of his hand.

"Huh?" Haruyuki reeled, captivated by the silver doors. "I-I'm going to open it?!"

"That *is* why you came, isn't it?"

"B-but it's not like I defeated the guard," he mumbled, his experience a month ago fresh in his mind. He had slipped into the Castle main building with Utai, using the window Chrome Falcon opened long, long ago to get inside, so he had never even approached the main entrance before. Wondering if he was really qualified to open the doors, he looked up at the magnificent entryway.

"Aah, enough! I grow impatient!" It was, of course, the Archangel Metatron shouting. The small, three-dimensional icon moved from Haruyuki's shoulder to above his head and slapped at his helmet with her wings. "This is an order, servant. Open those doors immediately! Come on, hurry it up!"

"G-got it." He quickly placed a hand on each door, and without taking a moment to savor the occasion, he pushed with all his might on the metal panels, feeling their heavy density.

Fortunately, he was not confronted with the humiliating tragedy of pushing on a door only to find he was supposed to pull; no, this time, the large doors began to open outward, the ground rumbling sonorously. Cool air flowed out from the darkness inside, and he suddenly felt all eight thousand years of the Accelerated World keenly.

Once the double doors were all the way open, several pale flames sprang up ahead of him to clear away the darkness and reveal a vast entrance hall. On the far side were broad stairs leading upward, and a number of doors were set in the walls to either side. There was no sign of Enemies inside, but the aura of the guards at the top of the stairs or lying in wait behind the doors mixed with the cold air and rolled out over his feet.

However, only Haruyuki was so nervous he couldn't speak; his comrades casually crossed the threshold and proceeded inside. And then Metatron started whapping him on the head again, so he hurried after them.

"Okay then." Graphite Edge stopped and looked around, after he'd led them forward for a minute or so. "Where's safe ground in the Moonlight stage again?"

"Oh, it's not this hall?" Fuko asked. "There don't appear to be any Enemies."

The double sword user shrugged. "Unfortunately, every five minutes, a patrolling Enemy comes in through some door. We can't really relax and talk here."

"So then you should have defeated all the Enemies inside," she replied.

"Whoa, whoa. Don't get carried away," he protested with a cheeky grin. "We didn't have time for that. We had to really hustle to get them cleared away outside."

Fuko narrowed her eye lenses, and Haruyuki knew why. So Graph and Lead *had* known when Haruyuki and Fuko appeared in the Unlimited Neutral Field and had made preparations to welcome them…

The swordmaster squirmed under Fuko's hard gaze until he was rescued by Lead.

"Master, I'm pretty sure the safe area was the small room at the top of the stairs."

"Ohhh, right, right, right." Graph fumbled cheerfully as he began to move again.

It appeared that the student had a firmer mental map of the interior of the main building than the master.

Now that he was thinking about it, Haruyuki hadn't seen Graph here at all the last time. Of course, it wasn't like he was diving 24-7, but the same could be said for his student Trilead, despite the fact that today wasn't the first time Trilead had appeared with exquisite timing. The last time Haruyuki was here, Trilead had suddenly been there when Haruyuki and Utai first met him in the Arc hall somewhere in the depths of this building. How on earth were they sensing people coming into the Unlimited Neutral Field? Haruyuki was caught up in the mystery as he cut across the entrance hall after the three other Burst Linkers.

Once they had climbed the large staircase, they came to a long hallway stretching out straight ahead, once again with any number of doors in both walls. Even if they wanted to open every door and check inside, it would take far too long, but Trilead walked over to the second door on the left without hesitation and quietly pulled it open.

Assuming an Enemy would leap out roaring, Haruyuki flinched reflexively. But in the end, there was none of that—the young samurai simply urged them to step through the door and into a long, narrow hallway that led to a square room about six meters on each side. Lead had said it was a small room, but in real-world measurements, it was about thirty square meters. Made entirely of stone, the room was windowless, but the lamps hanging on all four walls gave off more than enough light. There was a wooden table in the center, and as if the room had been made to order, four chairs sat around it.

"No tea to offer, but, well, have a seat anyway," Graphite Edge said. He set himself down first, and Lead took the seat next to him.

Haruyuki exchanged a look with Fuko before sitting down across from the other Burst Linkers. Instantly, he felt the tension that had kept his nerves taut since the moment they started out for the Suzaku gate spill out of him, and he let out an unconscious sigh. Metatron also floated down from his head back to his shoulder.

But he couldn't relax yet. There were still so many things that he had to do—that he had to learn. Sitting up straight, he first opened his Instruct menu and checked their accumulated dive time. The display read fifty-five minutes. Haruyuki and Fuko had set the safety so that it would automatically disconnect after one hour, fifty-six minutes and forty seconds of inside time, so they had about an hour left. If they couldn't achieve their goal before then, they would have to return to the real world and immediately reaccelerate.

"We don't have a lot of time, so please speak quickly, Graph,"

Fuko began immediately as she closed the Instruct menu she'd opened at the same time as Haruyuki. "First, how did you unlock the Genbu gate seal and enter the Castle? Start there."

"Hmm. Hmmmm..." Arms crossed, Graphite Edge groaned for a bit before nodding as though he'd made up his mind about something. "Well, I *did* leave Denden and the rest of you hanging, so I'll tell you everything I can. But I'm still a member of GW, so I can't exactly go spilling that stuff. You gotta understand that."

"...Fine," Fuko assented briefly.

When the curtain fell the other day on the mock Territories against Great Wall in Shibuya No. 2, Nega Nebulus had won. As a result, the Green King himself had promised to return Shibuya Areas Nos. 1 and 2, but he had not extended this promise to include Graphite Edge's return to Nega Nebulus's Four Elements. This was because, in joining the ranks of Great Wall back in the day, Graphite Edge had taken the role of stanching the blood and bearing the brunt of the dissatisfaction likely to erupt among the Legion members over the abrupt loss of their territory. It was unclear exactly how he would pacify them, but at the very least, he apparently had no intention of betraying his position and responsibilities as first seat of the Six Armors.

He moved his hand from his chest up to his right shoulder and grabbed hold of the hilt stretching out there.

*Chank!* The instant the sword was unsheathed, Haruyuki hovered up above his seat slightly. But Fuko simply watched calmly, so he hurried to reseat himself.

Graph stretched out the hand with the sword before him and set his weapon down on the table gently. "This guy's one part of my initial and final equipment, Lux."

Haruyuki stared wordlessly at Graphite Edge's legendary Enhanced Armament up close for the first time. He had seen more than a few sword-type Enhanced Armaments up to that point, but the particular form of this one made it stand out from all the rest. Most impressive was the blade itself, so transparent it almost didn't exist at all, jet-black coloring wrapped around it like a frame. The blade was eighty centimeters long and probably eight millimeters thick. Its ephemeral beauty made it seem more like a piece of art than a weapon, but Haruyuki had seen in the earlier battle that this sword was a match for the Black King's own Terminate Sword.

Fuko, meanwhile, seemed utterly unimpressed as she lifted her chin. "And what of it, your true self on the table here?"

Instantly, a giggle slipped out of Lead. Graph also shrugged as though he were smiling wryly before speaking again.

"It's not like I'm trying to brag, okay? But um, at best, this is just an item with particular settings. The edge is made of this stuff graphene, though. And graphene is as thick as an atom of carbon…Meaning you can think of this sword as being 'honed to single atom,' the way you see in old manga and anime all the time."

"Ohh…"

*Cool!* Haruyuki thought innocently, letting out an admiring hum.

Fuko simply urged him to continue with a nod.

"Okay, so this is totally different from that. Crow…and whoever's on your shoulder there, you've gotten the lecture about the Incarnate system, yeah?"

Haruyuki glanced at his Incarnate technique instructor—or rather the teacher from hell that was Fuko—before hurriedly nodding. Metatron also flashed her angel halo once to indicate her agreement.

"Great. Put simply, the Incarnate System is a technique to interfere with the game using the power of one's imagination. So long as your imagination's strong enough, you can do things that are set as impossible in the system. And conversely, you can stop being able to do things that had previously been possible. The first one's overwriting, and the second's Zero Fill. Basically, you can do stuff like punch holes in indestructible terrain or make a totally close-range type use super-long-range techniques."

"In other words, Graph, is this what you're trying to say? That you used that sword and Incarnate techniques to break the Castle's north gate?" Fuko asked suspiciously, eyebrow raised.

"No, no." The dual swordmaster immediately shook his head. "Use Incarnate all you want, but that ain't gonna happen. The ninefold gate that guards the Castle—the four gates in the four cardinal directions, the main doors of the main building, and then the four massive doors inside—are top-priority objects in the Unlimited Neutral Field. To smash 'em with Incarnate would be totally out of the question, even for Vanquish's rage-gauge explosion status."

Vanquish, aka the Blue King, Blue Knight, was said to be the most powerful close-range type in the Accelerated World. If *he* couldn't do it, then there wasn't a Burst Linker in the world who could destroy the four gates. In that case, however, what exactly did Graphite Edge *do* with his sword and Incarnate technique?

"Listen, Graph. I told you we don't have a lot of time. Perhaps you could get to the point sooner rather than later." Fuko was about three times as patient as the impatient alien Pard, and even she had a note of annoyance creeping into her voice as she admonished him.

But the swordsman remained irritatingly carefree. He lifted the sword once more and said, in fond reminiscence, "I taught Lota three types of Incarnate techniques: Vorpal Strike, Starburst Stream, and The Eclipse. They're all showy, high-power, second-stage attacks. But like...with the Incarnate System, there's something beyond that."

"What?!" Haruyuki cried out once again. He stared intently at the swordmaster's face mask as he asked, oh so timidly, "S-so that would be...third-stage Incarnate techniques then?"

"Mmm." Casually assenting, Graph began to explain, moving Lux like a pointer. "I'll go over the deets just in case. First-stage Incarnate techniques are just one type—range, movement, power, or defense expansion. Like, the basics. Second stage combines the different types, or else they're adapted techniques that give results outside the standard framework. Good so far, yeah?"

Haruyuki bobbed his head up and down, Metatron made her halo flash, and even Fuko dipped her head slightly.

"Great. So, to sum it all up, second stage's like way flashier than first. So then, third stage oughtta be all *bang* and *pew-pew...* That's what you'd think, right, Crow?"

His name suddenly called, Haruyuki went ahead and nodded.

Graph leaned back, seemingly satisfied, and swung the sword from side to side. "Actually, truth is, it's kinda the opposite."

"Wh-whaaaaat?!" *So then why did you push that on me before?!* Haruyuki wanted to voice his complaint, but his interest in the topic won out. "Opposite...So then, third-stage techniques are smaller and less conspicuous than second...Is that it?"

"That is totally, exactly it. Still, that doesn't mean they're weak. Just the opposite, in fact...it's like that thing. In manga and stuff, they're always like 'First you go big, and then you bring it home,' y'know? In the third stage, you take the imagination you expanded waaaay out in the second stage and focus it on a single point, like, to an extreme. As for what happens when you do, well—" Graph had simply rambled on and was starting to puff his chest out for his next line when he was cut off by a voice from Haruyuki's shoulder.

"Direct interference with the information on the Highest Level."

The swordsman stopped as if stunned.

"That *is* what you are attempting to explain, is it not, Graph or whatever it was?"

"...Well, this is a shocker..." Perhaps he wasn't just saying it and really was surprised; Graph simply focused on the 3-D icon for an intent moment, speechless. Finally, he nodded slowly, as if coming to an understanding. "I really feel like I met Shoulderina there somewhere a really long time ago. It's not a Burst Linker sensory terminal, though, is it? An Enemy…and one of the highest class, the Legend class. So one of the Four Divines?"

"You do have fairly decent eyes, then. You are quite right."

Realizing that now that it had come to this, and it would be impossible to fool Graph, Haruyuki let the small icon proudly name herself.

"I am the master of Silver Crow, the ruler of the Contrary Cathedral, one pillar of the Four Divines, the Archangel Metatron."

After a few seconds of silence, Trilead was first to bow politely. "I apologize for the lateness of my greeting. I am called Trilead Tetroxide, and I am Graphite Edge's student."

"Mmm. I shall remember this," Metatron replied placidly as she turned her icon toward Lead's master and awaited his greeting as well.

But the twin blades swordsman simply stammered—"Ah, ah, ah"—and rather rudely pointed at the icon. "Okay, okay, I get it now. So *that's* why I felt like I knew you somehow. Waaay back when, I fought you, just the one time," Graph said, as though fondly reminiscing. "I worked so ridiculously hard to take you down, and then the Arc altar was empty, so it was pretty sad, though."

Metatron made an angry "hmph" before rattling on smoothly in a very non-AI-like way. "You sound proud when you say you defeated me, but what you were in contest against was nothing more than my first form. And you also had the support of a Hell stage; if we fought outside the Castle, a mere warrior such as yourself would not last a hundred seconds against me. The same could be said for the warrior who came a little earlier than you and took The Luminary out from my palace."

"R-right. Sorry for talking big," Graph apologized, chastened, and cleared his throat. "Um, so…what was I talking about again…?"

"The third-stage Incarnate techniques, Master," Trilead noted.

"Right, that." He nodded solemnly. "Still, it's just like Ms. Archangel there said, you can sum up the important part in a few

words—'Manipulating phenomenon from a higher dimension.' …If you can completely master this stage, then distance becomes irrelevant."

Instantly, something Metatron had said to him popped up in the back of Haruyuki's mind:

*Listen to me, little warrior. On the Highest Level, the concept of "distance" is meaningless. Thus, it is possible for us two to touch like this, despite the fact that we are far apart on the Mean Level; for us to have this overview of all three fields; and to even reference memories…*

The concept of distance didn't exist on the Highest Level. If it did…

"Uh, um, so then, that means…You can attack anything, and it doesn't matter where it is or how far away?" Haruyuki asked timidly. "Unilaterally strike an opponent a few dozen kilometers away from you?"

"Taken to the extreme, that's what it ends up being," Graph agreed. "And it's not just distance. Attack power, defensive abilities, compatibility—all parameters get tossed out the window. You could even do something like completely and utterly destroy the entire field with a toy gun. Anyone who totally conquers the third stage'd basically be a god of this world."

"A-a god?"

"Yeah. It'd be like they got administrator privileges…"

Sensing pain in Graphite Edge's voice as he spoke half to himself, Haruyuki blinked hard and stared. But no matter how he focused on the dual swordsman's goggles, looking for the eye lenses hidden beneath, he couldn't read what was going on inside the avatar's head.

Haruyuki shifted his gaze to the longsword still gripped in Graph's right hand and asked another question. "So then, is it…? You mastered this third-stage Incarnate technique and broke through the Castle's north gate?"

"Hmm. The answer's eighty percent no and twenty percent yes, I guess." Casually carefree again, the swordmaster shrugged lightly. "If I had the power to do that, forget the gate; I'd have been able to take down the God at it, yeah? But there's totally no way I could do that. I'm still real far from mastery. And you can't escape the core of the Incarnate—its biggest principle, the fact that the imagination comes from your mind. You always end up bound by the frame of your own self."

"And how, finally, does this relate to your earlier talk of graphene, pray tell?" Fuko spoke for the first time in a while.

"Ri-ri-right." Graph moved his face mask up and down slightly. "Rekka's always saying I'm more sword than person, and she's not necessarily off base there. If G—if the Green King's the Burst Linker in our world going the extra mile to protect people, then I'm the one who's thought about nothing but cutting. So you know, I'm not too shabby with Incarnate. And I've focused and concentrated that to my limits, for this third-stage Incarnate technique."

Graphite Edge dropped his gaze to the long sword clutched in one hand, and a hazy, bluish-purple overlay rose up from his body. The overlay was the extra noise from the excess of imagination flowing into the image-control circuits that connected a Burst Linker's mind and their avatar; the system processed it as a light effect. The overlay enveloping Graph currently was subdued, but probably not because his Incarnate level was low. The opposite, in fact—because his imagination was so purely honed and refined, it caused virtually no noise.

Clink. The longsword Lux vanished with a crisp metallic sound.

No, not vanished…The sword had become as thin as humanly possible, sinking down to the atomic level. The hazy, shadowy blade would disappear and reappear when Haruyuki shifted his head to change the angle he viewed it at.

Now that the sword was indeed "honed to the thickness of a single atom," Graph stood up from his seat, hand still on the grip. He looked back and then swiftly swung his sword away from the other Burst Linkers there.

There was no call of a technique name. Just the flashing movement of his right arm, three times. He then sheathed the sword and took a step back.

A second later, a triangle-size area of the stone floor sank down. Graph had severed the supposedly indestructible foundation of the Castle. The block continued to sink, gradually dropping out of the floor, and a few moments later, they heard the sound of two heavy objects colliding.

"So, basically, that's the idea." Graphite Edge turned around and spread his hands.

"Now listen, Graph." Fuko was half stunned, half exasperated. "Before, you said—the 'ninefold gates,' was it? You said it was absolutely impossible to destroy the Castle's four directional gates. This demonstration contradicts that. Can't you simply use that technique to open a hole in the large door at the gates?"

"I tried that, at first. But the gates rejected even a third-level Incarnate technique. They probably use up a tremendous amount of resources to constantly update their data. But there is *one* gap we can exploit. Listen. Those gate doors themselves are indestructible, but the double doors and the others, they have gaps in their logical openings."

Graph thrust his palms forward, as if making contact with each of the double doors. "The width of this gap is infinitely close to zero. But the thickness of the atomic blade I produce with my Incarnate technique is also infinitely close to zero. So there's wiggle room for me to push the 'logic' of my Incarnate technique. Of course, it's pointless if my blade makes it through when I can't… But with the four directional gates, it's enough if just my blade can pass through. Because—"

"You can destroy the seal plate from outside the gate!" Haruyuki shouted.

"Exactly." Graph seemed to be grinning as he opened his hands. "I said this before, but in short, third-stage Incarnate is about pushing through to the result. The argument that you believe is absolute—I call it the absolute theory. And with it, you can overwrite things whether anyone likes it or not. There's no flashy lights or big explosions; you simply get the results.

"The absolute theory behind Elucidator is that this blade is thin and sharp to the extreme, so it can cut anything. It doesn't work on the ninefold gates themselves, but I managed to slip the blade through the gap and cut the seal. Wasn't as easy as I make it sound, though."

That was obviously true. If you were going to try to pass a blade with zero thickness through a gap with zero width, then the tolerance for error would also be zero. And on top of that, you would have to slice through the solid seal plate with one hit, which would require swinging with full force at top speed.

"So you made it work with one hit?" Haruyuki asked, half disbelieving.

"No way." Graph wove his hands back and forth to indicate a negative. "I failed so many times, got massacred by Genbu so many times...But in the Unlimited Neutral Field, you've got time if nothing else, and I had a bunch of extra points. I focused on the challenge like I was in training, and right around the time I forgot how many times I'd died, I finally made it work."

"Graph, if you had enough points that you could die that many times, then why didn't you try to flee to the other side of the bridge instead of inside the gate?" Fuko asked, exasperated.

"Nah, there was no way." He shook his head once again. "I had about three seconds leeway from the time I regenerated on the bridge until Genbu popped up to attack me. But about fifty percent of the time, that turtle comes barreling at you with the gravity attack on its first go. No matter how far you get before that, you just get sucked back and have to start all over again. Swinging my sword at the gate in front of me was way more constructive. And..." He looked down at Lead, sitting properly on the chair to his left. "And because I made it inside the Castle, I managed to get my second student. All my hard work wasn't for nothing."

*Right.* Hearing this, Haruyuki belatedly remembered the sword wielder before him was Kuroyukihime's teacher, and Kuroyuki-hime was Haruyuki's own swordmaster. Which meant Haruyuki was Graph's grand-student, and Graph would be Haruyuki's grand master. So then maybe he shouldn't be calling him Graph like he had been, but master, following Trilead's lead. Or maybe he should pick something else, like elder.

As Haruyuki sat sunk in thought, his other master—his Incarnate teacher, Sky Raker, let out a soft sigh. "My goodness, the first story is finally finished, hmm? That you would spend twenty minutes telling a tale that could've been finished with 'I broke through with an Incarnate technique.'"

"N-now you're just being mean, Rekka. I was doing my best to explain it, so it was easy for the young people and Ms. Archangel to understand."

"In my case, I comprehended the issue with simply 'I interfered from the Highest Level.'" Metatron's words were no less thorny and merciless than Fuko's, and Graph's shoulders slumped. Looking at this, Fuko smiled. "That's the first time you and I have agreed, Meta."

"Who are you calling 'Meta'?!" Metatron fumed, and Haru-yuki hurried to intercede.

"But, Metatron, you did say, right? That you can't interfere with comrades or enemies on the Highest Level. You can only recognize and be aware. I think it's the same with terrain, but…"

"It is admirable that you recollect my words, but if you are going to do so, then do so correctly. At that time, I said that *you* could not interfere. With your abilities in that moment in time, observing the Highest Level was your limit." Metatron's voice in cool declaration was just the slightest bit softer, something that Haruyuki alone likely realized. "But after that, you called to me through the Highest Level and reestablished the link that was nearly severed. If you do not call that interference, then what do you call it?"

"Oh…R-right…" Haruyuki remembered how, guided by a mysterious voice that gave its name as "something*terasu*," he had just barely managed to recover Metatron's core when she was on the verge of extinction, and he suddenly wanted to hug the icon on his shoulder. But if he did something like that, he had no doubt the surprisingly shy Archangel would be furious, so he resisted the urge and finished with a nod. "I had to concentrate so hard just to get my voice to finally reach you. I'm totally incapable of destroying something in the Highest Level."

"Of course, servant."

"Could I have a minute, Tron?" Fuko interjected again.

"Who are you calling 'Tron'?!"

"This Highest Level, if it's just looking, can anyone look, I wonder? For instance, myself?"

"…Mm…" Grunting with displeasure, Metatron moved from Haruyuki's right shoulder to his left and glanced at Fuko's avatar. "It is absolutely not the case that anyone can, but it would likely not be impossible for you. However. The reason Silver Crow was previously able to reach the Highest Level was because the calculation speed of his mental circuits increased dramatically during the battle with the pseudo-Being you call Mark II. To re-create that state in normal times would require long hours of concentration."

Haruyuki listened attentively to Metatron's slightly aggressive explanation, but fortunately, Fuko nodded, with no display of her own usual challenging spirit.

"I see. Well then, we will leave that for the next opportunity. The reason we have come to the Castle today is to obtain information on the seventh of the Arcs, The Fluctuating Light, and convey that to Black Lotus."

"Hmm. I am also greatly interested in this."

When Metatron agreed with her, Fuko turned back to Graphite Edge. "So then, shall we get on with the main discussion? Graph, given that you charged into this Castle three years ago, there's no way that you didn't investigate it. Tell me. What on earth is the final Arc?"

"H-hang on a sec." The dual swordmaster raised both his hands in protest.

"What, Graph?" Fuko's eye lenses flashed sharply. "Is there something you would rather not have known?"

"No, it's nothing like that." Eyes darting about, Graph looked as though he were turning something over in his mind, but he soon let out a sigh. "Fine, fine. I'll tell you whatever I know. About TFL and the secrets of the Accelerated World...But if I'm going to tell you all that, there's a more suitable place to do it."

"Where?" Fuko asked suspiciously, and the graphite swordsman snapped an index finger out, straight downward.

"The deepest part of this Castle main building, of course—on the other side of the last gate."

# 2

The six Great Legions known far and wide across the Accelerated World took their nicknames from the Kings of Pure Color who headed each of them, and they were often referred to by that nickname—Blue Legion, Green Legion, etc. However, this did not mean that, for instance, the Blue Legion was made up of only blue-type duel avatars, but there *was* a certain tendency for avatars similar to the Legion color to gravitate toward that Legion.

The exceptions were the White King and the still-small Black Legion. Given that the leaders of these Legions were rare and absolute colors, they were necessarily unable to attract similar types of avatars. At best, there was the somewhat whitish Ivory Tower, the White Legion's representative; and the somewhat blackish Graphite Edge, formerly of the Black Legion's executive. Compared with these two, the current Red Legion, Prominence, was, true to its name, made up of a good number of red types, despite its past near-collapse.

Blood Leopard aka Mihaya Kakei thought about this as she raced toward the main building of the Nerima Ward Office in Beast Mode. There was a rather ominous feel in the air in Nerima Area No. 3, where the special executive meeting would soon be held, because Mihaya, the starter for the duel, had gotten hit with a Thunder stage. Lightning flashed frequently deep in the black clouds that hung thick in the air, and a near-constant low rumbling echoed through the stage.

"Hope we'll be okay," the Red King, Scarlet Rain, aka Yuniko Kozuki, muttered from her back.

"Why?" Mihaya wondered briefly.

"Aah, the Thunder stage. You go up too high and you get zapped by the lightning and pretty much turn into charcoal, right? Just wondering if we'll be able to climb up to the roof of the ward office."

"...NP, I think."

"You *think*?"

"Pretty sure the height for lightning strikes is a hundred meters. The Ward office is about ninety meters."

"...So just barely..." Niko groaned.

Mihaya ran intently along Meijiro Street to the west. Ahead, the fifty-year-old ward building came into sight. When it was built, it had been the second tallest of the twenty-three ward offices, but it was currently faster to count up to it from the bottom of the height list. But the area around it still had no taller buildings, so the fact of its striking nature was unchanged.

She glanced at the timer and saw they still had 1,720 seconds left in the duel. She calculated that she had run the 1.5 kilometers from the cake shop Patisserie la Plage in Sakuradai to this point in eighty seconds. But the other two members of the executive said they would accelerate from the observation deck restaurant on the office's top floor, so they had long ago reached the roof. She turned left off of Meijiro, and the instant she slipped onto the ward office premises, Niko made a move to slide down off her back.

"Thanks, Pard. I can get the elevator now—"

"No need," she replied. "Acceleration burst."

"Whoa!" Niko cried, and Mihaya felt the smaller girl hurriedly wrap her arms around her neck as she jumped hard. The pads of her four paws stuck firmly to the perpendicular wall of the office building, and she started to run. As her level-seven bonus, she'd acquired the ability to run normally on any surface. Unlike her ability to run up walls, this did not use up her special-attack gauge, so she could climb even a one-hundred-meter building without fear that her energy would run out before she made it to the top, sending her plunging to the ground.

"Uh! So um! If you're gonna climb the walls, tell me first!" Niko complained.

"SRY." She finished climbing the smooth wall in a single breath and then held herself back from making a final, full-powered leap, even though that was what she wanted to do. There was a chance they could get caught in the range of the lightning if she did that, so she simply pulled them up over the edge and stopped.

The spacious rooftop heliport offered a perfect view of the urban landscapes of Nerima and Suginami unfolding under the uniform gray of the sky. When her gaze landed on Kannana Street, stretching out essentially due south, she saw a remarkably large skyscraper rising up in the distance.

Mihaya had gone by it any number of times—the condo of Silver Crow, aka Haruyuki Arita. But this was not the Unlimited Neutral Field, only a normal duel field, so she would be repelled by the stage boundary before she could make it all the way there. She brushed away the fleeting thought and returned her attention to the scene at hand.

Two figures were visible near the H mark in the center of the heliport. One was a rich purple and fairly large, while the other was a vivid reddish-purple and fairly small.

This time, Niko did manage to jump down off her back, and as she stretched dramatically, Mihaya chanted the command Shape Change. She shifted from the leopard form of Beast Mode back to the human shape of Normal Mode and approached the earlier arrivals.

"'Sup," she greeted.

"Unnnh," the larger M-type duel avatar to the right groaned, shaking the massive horns growing from both sides of his head.

"I *always* tell you this." The small F-type avatar to the left sounded exasperated. "You don't need to think up some catch-phrase greeting, Cassi. I mean, 'sup is basically just the same meaning as hey or something."

"No, I have an obligation to respond correctly. To what's asked of me. If I simply answer offhandedly, it will be the root of trouble later. So I will think for a while about how my own condition is. Please proceed."

The F-type avatar rolled her eyes at this overly formal response before turning back to Mihaya. "Cassi is as stupidly serious as always, but whatever. Rain, Pard, it's been ages, brahs! We're always on different teams in the Terries these days, so I bet you missed me, huh? Maybe today's special meeting is just 'cause you wanted to see my pretty face? Ah-ha-ha-ha!" Although her speech was casually masculine, her voice was sweetly sour and high, with a bit of a lisp, so listening to her speak so quickly was kind of dizzying.

Mihaya stopped herself from shrugging, while Niko, next to her, raised an easy hand as she greeted them. "'Sup, Cassi, Pokki. Sorry for making you come out all of a sudden. But it's not like I was all sad, y'know."

"As stubborn as ever, Rain. You actually just wanted to pat my fluffy fur, right? C'mon, here!" She darted over to Niko and rubbed up against her with her back, covered in fur-type armor, which was extremely rare in the Accelerated World. Although the Red King yanked herself backward at first, she gave in to the temptation and plunged both hands into the reddish-purple fur, moving them around roughly.

"Aah, there. Right there. Aah, your hands are so small, just perfect. Ah, a little higher."

"C'mon. Didn't you actually just want to be all fluffed up?" Even as she grumbled, Niko didn't stop moving her hands.

Mihaya had also petted the small avatar herself any number of times, and that fur was soft and smooth, honestly a first-rate texture. At least in general.

The official avatar name of the F-type Niko called Pokki was

Thistle Porcupine. Thistle from the plant—Porcupine, the animal. The common point being that both were thorny.

Thistle let out a groan as she moved away from Niko, perhaps in satisfaction from the plentiful back scratches, and the M-type behind them started to speak once again.

"When I assess my current state both in the physical and mental aspects, I find no major problems in terms of my health status, but I have been concerned about a slight pain in one of my back teeth for the past few days. On the other hand, my mental state is most certainly not poor because final exams are over, and it will be summer vacation soon. Thus, the answer to your earlier question is 'not bad,' Blood Leopard."

"Then say not bad right from the start! And go to the dentist!" Thistle groaned, the long fur on her back standing up slightly. "You get some nanomachines in there, that tooth'll be fixed in no time!"

"I have not overlooked this." The M-type threw his massive horns back. "After this congregation, I have an appointment... With the dentist by the station."

"Ohh, by the station? That place? Telling us all that, it's like you're asking us to come take a peek. This is a chance to crack you in the real, Cassi!"

"Ngh! Stop that! I am the type to strictly separate BB and the real!" The M-type—who appeared quite together but was occasionally not at all—was named Cassis Moose. Cassis was the plant, black currant, and moose was the large animal, so the naming pattern was exactly the same as Thistle. On top of that, the rich purple of their armors was also very similar. But that was where the similarities stopped. In addition to the horns, he had a massive frame and four sturdy limbs, with zero fur growing on his thick armor plates. Personality-wise, too, he could be said to have been a thinker amid the many impulsive types in the Red Legion—Thistle included.

Cassis Moose, Thistle Porcupine, and Blood Leopard were the executive group of Prominence, supporting the second Red

King. Since all three of their avatars were animal types, at some point, people started calling them by the nickname Triplex. But this sort of thing was apparently tradition with the seven major Legions.

Once they had finished saying hello, Mihaya shot Niko a glance before saying, "I'd like to get started then."

"Yeah, sure."

"Anytime."

Thistle and Cassis responded at the same time and instantly sobered. Both Thistle—with animal intuition—and Cassis—with advance information—had realized that the agenda for this special meeting was quite critical.

Mihaya usually took on the responsibility of leading their regular meetings, but today she yielded that position to Niko. Stepping forward to take her place, the Red King didn't speak right away, but rather looked wordlessly at each of the three members of the executive in turn. The small avatar, slightly smaller than Cassis and of the smallest class in the Accelerated World, suddenly seemed very large. "Cassi, Pokki, Pard. You remember the whole Cherry thing."

At this, Mihaya felt the air in the stage instantly grow even more tense.

Cherry Rook, Scarlet Rain's parent, had suddenly transformed into the fifth Chrome Disaster and attacked many Burst Linkers in the neutral areas in the vicinity of Ikebukuro. These included members of the other great Legions, who had concluded a mutual nonaggression treaty, and fearing that this would lead to strife among the Legions, Niko herself had directly contacted the just newly restored Black Legion, gained their assistance in subjugating Disaster, and banished Cherry Rook from the Accelerated World with her Judgment Blow.

"How could we forget?" Thistle muttered distinctly. She had been close with Cherry Rook, whose armor was not only a similar color to her own, but who also had an animal avatar name. "Crypt Cosmic Circus gave Cherry the Armor. The Acceleration

Research Society pulled the strings behind the scenes. I'll never forgive them for it." Her voice was quiet, but the fur on her back stood up silently. The long, fluffy bits of softness twisted together in strands of a dozen or so and began to transform into thick, sharp, striped spikes.

Niko nodded slowly and opened her mouth once again. "We'll definitely make Radio pay for that. But it's the Society we need to deal with first somehow. Just like I told you before, that gang's made a new armor, and they're about to come in and mess things up again with it. Not to mention that the base of it is my own Enhanced Armament thruster. Before the same thing happens again, we've got to get it back."

"Agreed. But, Rain, even if we wanted to strike first, we don't know who the Society really is. There's no way to attack." Thistle sounded annoyed, fur on her back still slightly standing. She still hadn't been told the greatest secret concerning the Acceleration Research Society.

Inside the black clouds that swirled so low that the avatars on the roof could almost reach out and touch them, something blinked faintly two or three times. After a second, the low rumble of distant thunder shook the ward office building.

"Pokki—Thistle," Niko corrected herself, using the other avatar's proper name, a strong light shining in her eye lenses. "First, I gotta apologize for not reporting this sooner. A little while ago, I met the leader of the Acceleration Research Society."

"Aaaaah. And?!" Thistle shouted. *Ping!* A single 50-centimeter needle shot up from her back and dug deep into the concrete surface of the heliport. "Th-the leader…Not that Black Vise guy who attacked you pretending to be the Black King, but the big boss above him?!"

"The big boss," Niko confirmed. "But that boss was a dummy avatar for watching, so…Still, even as a dummy, she was ready to take on Pard and me and the whole lot of Nega Nebulus. If we had fought…we probably wouldn't have won."

"Whaaaaaaa—?! You gotta be kidding!" *Ka-ting!* Two more

needles shot out and stabbed the floor. "But with that lineup, you had two kings, right?! No way a dummy could win!!"

"Nah." Niko shrugged. "Looks like she's a king, too, so."

"...Huh?" Thistle stopped dead in her tracks.

"The Acceleration Research Society boss is the head of Oscillatory Universe, the White King—White Cosmos."

"...Huuuuuuuh?!"

Mihaya watched as nearly ten needles shot out with this third scream and couldn't help but think *The real surprise is still coming. Save those needles.*

Fortunately, Thistle managed to get her cool back somehow, and after a few deep breaths, she looked back and forth between Niko and Mihaya. "So you're not kidding."

"Nah," Niko replied.

Mihaya nodded solemnly. The time the White King had appeared using a dummy avatar at Umesato Junior High (the Black Legion headquarters) was carved deep into her memory. Despite the fact that it had been a dummy, which only had the bare minimum of battle power, an overwhelming pressure had pushed down on her from above, and Mihaya had been unable to speak. But Niko, although she had likely been feeling the same thing, had brushed aside that terror and shouted, "You're the one pulling the strings here?"

She would never again be paralyzed in fear before Niko, not even up against the White King, not against Chrome Disaster, Mark II. Gritting her teeth with this resolve once more, Mihaya picked up the explanation from there. "The Acceleration Research Society hideout and the White Legion's headquarters are in the same place—the private Eternal Girls' Academy in Minato Area Three. Which means if the area stops being White territory, then there's a good possibility Society members will show up on the matching list."

"If we could confirm that, it's true that there wouldn't be any further doubt," Cassis Moose said, his voice ponderous. "It wouldn't be easy, however, to say the least. To strip them of their right to block the matching list, the only option is to defeat them. In the Territories, against the White Legion. Is that possible, in the Accelerated World now?"

"I don't know if it's possible. But they're willing to try." Mihaya took a breath. "This is totally top secret. In the Territories next week, Nega Nebulus is going to attack Oscillatory."

"Mmwhaaaaa—?!" Thistle Porcupine shrieked again, but this time, perhaps through self-restraint, none of the needles on her back went anywhere. "Attack...Negabu just got three new members, so they're barely ten people now?! So if they leave three to defend Suginami, the attacking team'll be, at most, seven. But Oscillatory's defending team'll be twice that—or in the worst case, three times! There's no way they're going to win!"

"Well, they intend to win, and they'll probably make a good show of it, at least," Niko said as a preamble, arms crossed, and drew closer to the main topic. "But I think it'll be a tough fight. Thinking about the worst case, there's no way Lotus herself can be a part of the attacking team. But this mission's a last chance for us in Prominence, too. To go up against the Society and get back my thruster, our only choice is to expose them here."

"I got a bad feeling about this, somehow," Thistle muttered.

Niko finally smiled at her, uttering the first of the meeting's main points. "So I was thinking we should be a part of Negabu's mission, too."

"...Nnmyug..." The strange sound the purplish porcupine made was probably from the effort of not shooting off all the needles on her back. She raised clawed hands before her, the upright needles on her back trembling. "H-hang on a sec. So like, Rain, I know you don't wanna be lectured or anything on the basic rules of the Territories at this point, but I'll just ask: Attacking teams in the Territories are in Legion units, so another Legion can't be a guest in the fight or anything. You know that, right?"

"Of course I know that." Niko's voice was stern.

A note of tension came up even on the capreoline face of the silent Cassis Moose. Thistle cast a glance at him before launching her second question. "So help, that means, like, we put up another team and attack Minato One or Two or something, yeah? But our territories aren't adjacent; we can't attack. Which means…one of us leaves the Legion temporarily and joins Negabu?"

"That's the basic idea. But…if we're all half-assed—'someone,' 'temporarily'—we'll never beat Oscillatory."

Perhaps anticipating the destructive power of the announcement Niko was about to make, the black clouds of the Thunder stage surged and twisted even more violently, and the low, heavy rumble of thunder echoed around them.

"Pard and I are gonna go help in the Territories," she finished.

The needles on Thistle's back stood up perfectly straight. "Mwah…?"

"But then Nerima's defense'll be unstable, so we're making it so we can call on help from Suginami at any time, too."

"Mwah…?!"

"If you're joking…"

*Koff!* After clearing her throat, the Red King gave voice to her final comment:

"Prominence and Nega Nebulus are going to merge."

"Mwaaaaaaaat?!" The shriek shook the duel stage, dozens of needles shot up into the air, and lightning bolts shot out of the sky one after the other, coloring the world in thunder and bright light.

# 3

Graphite Edge hadn't cut the hole in the floor for a mere demonstration. Having proposed that they change venues once more, the avatar walked over to the hole and pointed to it as he said, a little boastfully, "We go down through this hole. It should be a serious shortcut. But even still, to reach the hall of the Arc, we'll probably have to fight a couple guards."

Both of these guesses were correct. After jumping down the hole, the four of them only had to walk two hundred meters or so, but two Enemy guards stood in the middle of that path. The only way to get past was to fight, so the two high rankers—Graphite Edge and Sky Raker—showed what they were really made of, while Haruyuki and Trilead were little more than annoyances to the Enemies.

When they opened the large door that was the eighth of the ninefold gates and arrived at the large, gloomy hall, the accumulated acceleration time for Haruyuki and Fuko was ninety-five minutes. Just over twenty minutes left until the automatic disconnect safety was activated.

*I guess we'll have to go back there for a sec and then use another ten points to dive again,* Haruyuki thought as they cut across the hall, when two large daises appeared from the darkness ahead.

He approached in a near trot and went around to the front of the pedestal.

The two gleaming black stone pillars were separated by two meters. Silver plates were embedded on their fronts, never to lose their eternal shine. Inscribed on them was the Big Dipper and some Japanese characters, almost never used in the Accelerated World. The plate on the pedestal to the right read KAIYOU, while the one on the left said GYOKKO.

"These are the pedestals where the fifth and sixth Arcs were enshrined," Fuko murmured from where she stood next to him, seemingly moved.

"Yes, Master." Haruyuki nodded and added, "The armor on the right-hand pedestal was The Destiny, and the sword on the left pedestal was The Infinity. We sealed The Destiny away, but The Infinity is…"

He looked back at Trilead standing alongside Graph. The young warrior bashfully removed his straight sword from the sheath on his hip and gently raised it with both hands.

"This is The Infinity, Miss Raker. It is presumptuous of me, but I have taken possession of it. Would you like to hold it?"

"No, that's fine. It's a lovely sword. Thank you for showing it to me, Lead," Raker answered with a smile and then turned her gaze back to the pedestals. "Sword and…armor, then? They were in the Castle, so I assumed they would be patterned after the three sacred treasures, but it seems not, hmm?"

"The three sacred treasures? You mean from Japanese mythology?" Haruyuki cocked his head to one side.

Graphite Edge had snapped his fingers. "That's my professor, Rekka. You picked up on something good there. Lead and I've also talked about whether the Imperial regalia passed down through the Imperial family—the sword Kusanagi, the mirror Yata no Kagami, and the jewel Yasakani no Magatama—might correspond with the fifth, sixth, and seventh of the Seven Arcs in the Accelerated World."

"Goodness. But The Infinity is a sword, so even if it does follow from Kusanagi, The Destiny is armor, yes? Isn't it impossible for it to be patterned after the mirror?" Fuko's comment was entirely correct, and Haruyuki bobbed his head up and down.

But the dual swordsman waggled a finger back and forth. "On the contrary. Before it turned into the Disaster, The Destiny's true nature was to nullify physical attacks and reflect light-type attacks. More than anything else, it was a silver so bright it dazzled the eye, honestly like a mirror—"

"Goodness," Fuko interjected. "You talk as though you'd seen it."

Graph cleared his throat deliberately as he muttered evasively, "That is a thing in itself," before returning to his point. "At any rate. I think reading Destiny as corresponding to Yata no Kagami is not necessarily off base."

"S-so then…does that mean the third one, Yasakani no Magatama, corresponds to the seventh Arc…The Fluctuating Light?" The instant Haruyuki voiced this question, the icon on his shoulder, which had been silent for a while, flashed brightly for a mere instant. But it seemed she was not interested in actually saying anything, so he turned his eyes back to Graph.

The near-black avatar once again did not respond immediately. Silent, he turned slowly and looked at the northern wall of the great hall. It was shrouded in gloom, so Haruyuki couldn't really see it, but there was the black mouth of a gate there, with a design reminiscent of an ancient temple. The last of the ninefold gates. Unlike the other gates, it had no door, but a chill—rife with ill intent—flowed outward, not allowing any easy crossing of its threshold.

"The three imperial treasures enshrined in the imperial palace in the real world," Trilead said abruptly, causing Haruyuki to shift his gaze. The young samurai hung his sword from his left hip once more as he continued evenly, "Of the three, the sword and the mirror are *katashiro*; put more bluntly, they are replicas. The real Kusanagi is said to be at Atsuta Shrine in Aichi, while Yata no Kagami is supposedly at Ise Shrine in Mire. Yasakani no

Magatama is the only one actually set in the Kenji Hall at Fukiage Omiya Palace of the imperial court. Of course, I have not actually seen it."

"Which means that, of the three Arcs existing or having existed in the Castle in the Accelerated World, only the seventh, Youkou, is the real thing?" Fuko asked.

"I do not know by what means one would designate it as real." Trilead shook his head slightly. "But...Master Graph told me that it seems that of the kanji and English names given to the Seven Arcs, only Youkou and The Fluctuating Light correctly correspond."

"Huh? I know that the *kou* is *light*, but what does fluctuating mean?" Haruyuki cocked his head to one side ruefully. He should've looked it up in the dictionary before they came. He'd never heard the word before; at the very least, it wasn't an English word you learned in junior high.

It wasn't Trilead or Fuko who responded to Haruyuki's question, but Graphite Edge, gaze still focused on the ninth gate. "*Fluctuate* is a verb that means to sway, change, go up and down. Basically, fluctuating light means a light that shimmers and moves. Put it all together and you get Youkou."

Sensing something reflective in that as-ever lighthearted tone, Haruyuki blinked several times. But the swordmaster shrugged lightly as he turned around and continued, "I don't know if the fact that only the names of the final Arc correspond perfectly means anything...or if it's just a coincidence. If we wanna know, our only choice is to get to level ten and ask the developer or whoever directly." Graph laughed briefly.

"Graphite Edge, you should know this," came a laser-focused voice all of a sudden. "It is impossible that you—with the power to reach the Highest Level and the technique to enter Area Zero Zero—would not know this. The reason for the existence of Brain Burst, which you call the Accelerated World...It is in The Fluctuating Light."

The large white icon floated up, flashing remarkably brightly as she ordered the swordsman through the majestic voice of an archangel.

"Speak, Graphite Edge. Why are the little warriors of the three worlds, including the extinguished Accel Assault and Cosmos Corrupt, being made to fight? Why are we Beings given life? What is the final Arc, The Fluctuating Light?!"

Both Fuko and Trilead recoiled slightly in surprise. It was no wonder: They likely thought Metatron was at most an Enemy—an AI made to move by the BB system. But in the archangel's voice, there were echoes of the same struggle and longing that lived in the hearts of Haruyuki and the other Burst Linkers.

The swordsman didn't respond right away. He looked up at the tiny icon wordlessly as she floated slightly above his own head and then turned on his heel.

Eventually, a quiet voice came over his shoulder to them: "I said before, we should move to the Shrine of the Eight Divines before we talk about this."

He started to walk toward the ninth gate, and Metatron watched him silently. Finally, she slowly descended back to her position on Haruyuki's right shoulder.

After exchanging glances with Fuko and Lead, Haruyuki went after Graphite Edge. Once Silver Crow slipped through the solemn gates, a dense darkness filled his field of view, just like the last time. But he immediately saw the hazy light up ahead, and guided by the candle flame flickering in hollows in the walls, the party descended the spiral staircase that continued into the depths.

Haruyuki tried to count the number of steps this time, but he lost track right around a hundred. It was all he could do to simply resist the indescribable pressure that crawled along the icy stone steps. The reason it felt even more terrifying than it had a month ago was because he had more knowledge and experience, so that was fine, but…Mind racing, he intently put one foot after the other until finally Graph's voice rang out up ahead.

"We're here."

*Phew!* He let out a breath and lifted his head.

Every surface in the small room in the very depths of the Castle was covered in white tile, befitting the Moonlight stage. The light of the candlesticks reflected off the polished wooden floor, making it shimmer like the surface of water. The "small room" was actually about twice the size of the Arita living room. A large arch opened up on the wall in the back, but a slender silver fence barred passage through it. The opposite side was pitch-black.

Fuko cut across the room, her heels clacking lightly, to approach the fence fearlessly and face the darkness on the other side. Haruyuki walked timidly to her side and narrowed his eyes to gaze beyond the silver fence.

*Pok!* Abruptly, he heard the faintest of sounds, and a meager light grew some ways off. The source of the yellow light was a candle shimmering on top of an unfinished wooden platform. Similar lights lit up one after another in the depths ahead of them to outline a dim path.

Eventually, a black stone pedestal appeared in the distance.

It was the same as the ones in the hall above, but this one was not empty. On the pedestal, there was *something* enveloped in a pulsing blue light. A warm golden glow shimmered irregularly, as if tired of waiting for the moment when the seal would be broken.

"This is…the Shrine of the Eight Divines," Fuko murmured from next to Haruyuki.

"That is The Fluctuating Light," Metatron muttered on his shoulder.

"It really is a fluctuating light, hmm? From here, you can't tell what kind of item it is."

Fuko simply accepted it, while Metatron floated up slightly.

"It is very vexing that I can only observe visual spectrum data. Servant, Raker, approach it."

"Whoa! No way! There's no way!" Haruyuki shrieked immediately. "If we go past the sacred rope, powerful Enemies called the Eight Divines will appear, and it'll be a whole thing, right?"

This last query was directed at Trilead behind him. The young samurai nodded firmly and explained, "Yes. I have never seriously fought the Four Gods of the directional gates, but Master Graph has said that the battle power of the Eight Divines exceeds even their power."

"Is that so?" Fuko looked back at the swordsman leaning against the wall near the entrance.

"Mmm. Hmm." Scratching his helmet with a finger, Graph's answer was fairly evasive compared with his student's. "To be honest, I've only ever tried to run frantically from them and reach the pedestal without fighting. But it's like the Four Gods are, at best, massive Enemies on a fairly large battlefield. To put it in gaming terms, they're raid bosses. You can attack them all at once with a party of however many dozens of people, so you've got some wiggle room when it comes to strategies and techniques. But with the Eight Divines, as you can see, the battlefield is a room, and the enemy's about the size of a large duel avatar, so it's more PvP than boss fight—it's pretty close to Brain Burst's standard duel. If you're not careful, you'll have to fight one-on-one, but their specs are on the level of the Four Gods. My honest impression is that no one's getting anywhere with that."

"Hmm. If *you* are saying that, the person who challenged Inti solo, then I suppose we really aren't going to get anywhere," Fuko said.

With a wry smile, Graph shrugged.

Listening to this conversation between the two powerful and experienced high rankers, Haruyuki suddenly sensed a fundamental question. "Um, Graph," he said hesitantly. "Can I ask you something?"

"Hmm? What's up, Crow?"

"Um. Before, Metatron said that reaching the final Arc, The Fluctuating Light, was the reason that this game—that Brain Burst 2039—exists. So then, that means the creator of Brain Burst created the game to make us Burst Linkers break into the Castle. And it's a game, so I know you need to jump over all kinds of hurdles before you can get to the end. You level up, explore dungeons, get items, defeat bosses...But normally, there's a balance to the game, you know? Adjusting it to just the right level of difficulty is the creator's most important job, right? But...the Four Gods and the Eight Divines are absurdly powerful. It's almost like the creator doesn't want anyone to ever clear the game. So do they want us to invade the Castle or not? Honestly, which is it?"

Haruyuki had absolutely zero confidence in his ability to put his thoughts into words, but his interlocutor seemed to understand the question he had so earnestly put forth.

The double swordsman slowly nodded and spoke in a more serious tone. "Silver Crow. Your impression that the settings of this game are contradictory is entirely correct. But there's nothing to be done about that. Because Brain Burst 2039 is both a game and not a game."

"What...does that mean?" Haruyuki asked, holding his breath. He'd had basically the same question about the Highest Level when the Archangel Metatron showed it to him in the middle of the battle at the headquarters of the Acceleration Research Society at the end of the previous month.

If the creator of Brain Burst placed TFL in the deepest depths of the Castle, then all they had to do was reach out and take it with the hand of God if they needed it again, right? They could set anything as the game-clear marker; why did they have to go out of their way to make countless Burst Linkers attack the Castle?

Graphite Edge stirred slightly before him, but before the man could speak, Fuko raised her hand to stop him. "Wait. There's only two minutes left before Corvus and I automatically disconnect. This seems like it will be a long story, so can we continue once we dive back in?"

"Aah. Right. Okay, Lead and I'll wait around here, so log in—I mean, dive again as soon as you can," Graph said in his usual carefree tone, for some reason mixing in ancient net game terms, and crossed his arms, still leaning back against the wall.

Haruyuki glanced at the total time in his Instruct menu, which he'd left open all this time, before muttering to the 3-D icon on his shoulder, "Sorry, Metatron. We'll be back soon, so just wait a sec, okay?"

"Do not tarry, servant." While Metatron sounded as arrogant as ever, there was also the slightest bit of a sulk in her voice, and he grinned at this as he bowed to Trilead, who had moved to stand next to Graph.

"Lead, we're just going to go back for a bit."

"Yes, take your time, Crow. Miss Raker."

Once they had finished their good-byes, they had thirty seconds left. He and Fuko nodded at each other and readied themselves for the disconnection when, abruptly, Graph snapped his fingers.

"Oh, right, Rekka! Make the next safety activation time around ten hours."

"That's quite long," she remarked

"There's a reason for that. So please and thanks."

Fuko looked slightly suspicious, but she nodded, and a second after she gripped Haruyuki's hand, a warning shone bright red in his field of view.

DISCONNECTION WARNING—beyond the row of letters, the Castle depths melted into the light and disappeared.

# 4

"Mah…mah…ma-ma-ma-ma-ma-ma-ma-ma-ma-ma." Stammering like a broken sound file, Thistle Porcupine was transformed at once into a cute, round animal, having fired every single needle on her back.

Cassis Moose clapped a large hand lightly on her back, and Thistle coughed for a moment or two before sucking air into her lungs.

"Merrrrrrge?!" she shrieked at double-decibel volume.

*Kreeeeenk!*

Mihaya waited for the earsplitting sound to fade away and then nodded with Niko.

"Yes."

"That's right."

Thistle staggered backward. Of the three members of the Triplex, she had been the most concerned about any form of cooperation with Nega Nebulus, so her shock was entirely understandable, but they had to get her to agree before the meeting was over.

"No." Although her torso was still thrown back at a twenty-degree angle, her feet had stopped shuffling away from them. Thistle thrust her hands out ahead of her and shook her head back and forth. "No-no-no-no. Hang on a sec. Um. To begin with, is it even possible system-wise to merge Legions?"

"Yes." Mihaya nodded at the porcupine as she finally started to calm down a bit. "But for a merger between Legions that both have territory, their territory has to be adjacent."

"So then what happens to the Legion name and the Legion Master?" she asked immediately.

"You can pick and choose, I guess," Niko replied. "Keep one of the Legion names or pick a new one or something. And both LMs can stay on as is, or you can pick someone new."

"Hmm." Thistle considered this. "What about those kids from Setagaya who joined Negabu whenever that was?"

"Oh, that wasn't a merger," Niko told her. "They disbanded their original Legion and formally joined Negabu."

"Huh? Why'd they go through all that hassle?"

"Dunno. I didn't get that part of the story."

Thistle and Niko cocked their heads to one side in unison.

"Balance, probably," Cassis Moose said, breaking his silence. "With the Judgment Blow."

"Whaddya mean?" Thistle cocked her head to the opposite side.

"I only discovered this when I looked into it now. Regardless of what options are chosen, when two Legions merge, both of the original Legion Masters continue to possess that right for one month. The right to activate the Judgment Blow."

"Whoa." Thistle whistled. "So then, if the merged Legion chooses a totally new master, with the two former Masters, there'd be three people who could Judge?"

"It would appear so," Cassis agreed.

"Whoa-ho. You get a big fight going after the merger, and it'll be a Judgment festival!"

"That's not a festival I want to go to," Niko interjected with a smirk. "So then, the Petit Paquet LM went and disbanded the Legion so she wouldn't still have the right to Judge? That takes some real guts."

"Hey, hey, hey, heeey! Now's not the time for getting all starry-eyed, Rain!" Thistle started to get worked up again, her voice rising in pitch. "There's no way we're gonna be doing that, right?! I'm not here for that, not that kinda one-sided, take-it-all merger!!"

"Calm down, Pokki." Cassis placed both hands on Thistle's shoulders, and the small porcupine gradually cooled down once again.

She let out a long breath and stared up at the larger moose. "You're way too calm, Cassi...Oh! Or maybe you knew about the merger right from the start?!"

"N-no, don't worry about that." Clearing his throat, Cassis removed his hands and took a step back.

Thistle Porcupine's guess was correct. Before this meeting, Mihaya and Niko had sounded out Cassis Moose alone on the possibility of merging Legions. They'd done so because Thistle's flash point was famously low, and they'd wanted him to pacify her. But he'd apparently taken the opportunity to dig a little deeper on his own into what the whole thing would mean.

His cool powers of judgment and Thistle's nimble explosive force had saved them any number of times in the short period that they'd fought together as Submasters of the new Prominence. Both were essential members of the top executive and loved Prominence very deeply. That love was maybe even greater than Mihaya's own.

Mihaya's loyalty as one of the Triplex was more deeply focused on Niko personally rather than the Legion. And her passion as a Burst Linker was turned more toward individual battles than the Territories. The reason she frequented the so-called duel holy land, Akihabara Battle Ground, was to gather information, but another big factor was her desire to refine her one-on-one duel techniques. Thus, she didn't feel any serious resistance to the idea of merging with Nega Nebulus. Of course, it was a shame that the Prominence name would be gone, but as long as Niko was there, the new space would be Mihaya's battlefield. And anyway, Niko had decided on the current merger policy only after a lot of wrestling with the idea.

But the majority of Prominence members wouldn't be able to accept it as easily as all that. Even Thistle, who had risen to the top during the rule of the second King, was deeply shocked, so veteran members from the time of the first king, like Blaze Heart and Peach Parasol, would be more than surprised. After all, it had been the current Legion Master of Nega Nebulus, Black Lotus, who had taken the head of the previous Red King, Red Rider, and pushed him to total point loss.

"Pokki. I get that a merger with Negabu's a tough sell." Niko, speaking softly, turned toward Thistle Porcupine, whose lavender fur silently rippled as it regenerated. "Of course, I'm not thinkin' we'll just disband Promi and get sucked up into Negabu. I'm gonna seriously negotiate so that it's an equal merger. But... even still, to be honest, I doubt all the current Legion members'll follow me. I'm expecting any number of them to leave, and...If you or Cassi make that choice, I don't have the right to hold that against you."

Thistle opened her mouth, ready to fire back instantly once more, and once again, Cassis gently pressed down on her shoulders to silence her. Niko kept her gaze squarely on them as she continued.

"But...I've been thinking a lot lately. Like, after my predecessor was retired, why'd we fight so desperately to stay alive in Nerima and Ikebukuro during the total chaos of the warring states period? I'm up here, sitting on the throne as the second Red King, so what am I doing gritting my teeth and protecting our territory? I'm totally no good at bringing together huge forces, and to be honest, I don't feel too much of an attachment to the Prominence name. Like, I'd be happy with a few close pals in a tiny Legion with no territory or nothing, just hanging out in a corner of the Accelerated World, y'know?"

The small crimson avatar looked up at the cloudy sky of the

Thunder stage. She slowly pointed with one hand as though she had spotted a bird flying in the thick, distant clouds.

"I know it wasn't that I wanted to run away. Not from that lot who came and attacked us, like they were gonna earn big points from the Red Legion when we were on the verge of destruction. Not from those jerks in the major Legions who looked down on me like I wasn't a pure color after all, like I was a fake king. And not from the members of Promi now, not when they rely on me for real. But I've sorta been bluffing my way through this, like any second the paint's gonna peel off, and everyone'll see that I'm actually awful; and that's so scary I can hardly stand it. But still, in my heart, I'm totally certain of it; I don't want to run, and I don't want to lose."

It almost certainly wasn't Mihaya who had brought about this realization in Niko, but rather the silver corvus she'd met only six months ago. Equal parts sad and happy about this, Mihaya turned her ears toward her young Legion Master's speech so as not to let a single word get away from her.

"So I want to stand my ground now. To be honest, the Acceleration Research Society and the White Legion scare the heck outta me. But they did Cherry in...So they're my enemy, too. If I run away now and leave it all to the Negabu gang, I won't have any right to call myself a king anymore. This time, for sure, I want to fight for the sake of the things I hafta protect. That's why...I'm asking you, Pokki, Cassi. Help me." Niko bowed deeply toward the two members of the Triplex.

A large ripple ran through fully regenerated fur, and Thistle took a deep breath before asking their Legion Master in a low voice, "And what is it that you 'hafta protect,' Rain?"

"Myself, my Promi comrades...and this Accelerated World itself," Niko answered unwaveringly as she stood up straight once again.

Cassis shook his massive horns once. "The Black King has her sights set on level ten—on clearing the game Brain Burst. Your will to fight alongside her isn't shaken even if the path she walks will lead to the end of the Accelerated World?"

"Yeah. That's the thing she's gotta protect and all. And I don't think this world'll suddenly vanish or anything just because one person makes it to level ten. I mean, we go up levels to win something, yeah? If this game was so sad you could clear it just by getting a bigger number, then we wouldn't be so desperate like this, laughing and crying and whatnot. Even if someone does make level ten and meet the developer or whoever, they'll just get a new quest or mission or something, and that'll be the end of it," Niko declared.

Mihaya had also started to feel the same way, with apologies to the Black King. But on the other hand, she wasn't quite firm enough in that feeling to state that Brain Burst level ten was a mere number. Because, among all the levels, it was only level ten that couldn't be reached by earning some particular number of Burst Points. Only a player who had driven five other level niners to total point loss and walked that blood-soaked path could reach the unknown land of level ten.

Niko called this conquering path of personal supremacy the Black King was on "something to protect." She must have seen something of her own self inside the Black King. They differed in that one had guns and the other, swords, but both duel avatars hurt everyone and everything that came near them, and both had been born with the ability to keep others at a distance. They were also both trying to face this power—the manifestation of their own mental scars—head-on and accept it. They wanted to transform their scars into strength—the darkness into the light.

"So like...even if the time comes when I gotta fight Lotus someday..." As Niko looked at the silent members of the Triplex in turn, her eye lenses shone with a powerful light. "Even if one of us ends up at total point loss, I'll accept that fate. I mean, *I'm* the one who chose to go up to level nine even though I knew about the sudden-death rule, y'know? ...I sought power 'cause I wanted to protect the world around me. So I want to see that decision through, right to the end. And to protect the things I wanna protect, right now that means I hafta join forces with Lotus and fight the White Legion."

For a while, neither Thistle nor Cassis said anything. Thistle's fur flew up on end briefly before falling back down, soft against her back, a cool breeze making it ripple and wave.

The thistle-colored duel avatar stared up at the swirling black clouds and slowly nodded. "I guess if you're ready to go that far, Rain, we got no choice but to stick with you right up to the end. Lemme talk to Blaze and them old-timers. I'm pretty sure they'll get on board if we sit down and hash it out." Her voice held equal parts concern over an uncertain future, fear of a powerful enemy, and the resolve possessed only by one who has chosen to fight.

Cassis Moose also assented, his nod making his heavy armor clank. "I thought it would come at some point…the time to leave the territory and fight. It's in an unexpected form, but I will also follow our Legion Master's will."

Hearing their declarations, Niko nodded firmly in return and thrust a clenched fist out in front of her. "Thanks, Pokki, Cassi… and Pard. No matter how things change from here on out, I promise you this, at least: I'm definitely not running away. Up against the White King or the Armor of Catastrophe, Mark II, or whoever, I'm never freakin' out or steppin' back. I'm gonna fight with everything I got right up until the end."

Thistle and Cassis approached her wordlessly and bumped Niko's small fist with their own clenched hands.

*You've gotten stronger, huh, Niko?* Mihaya murmured internally, touching her own fist to the others.

A small gap in the black clouds of the Thunder stage opened up, and the light that poured down through it made their four fists glitter and shine like rising flames.

# 5

Waking up in the living room of the Arita house in the real world, Haruyuki had no sooner opened his eyes than he was lifting his hand to access the settings screen of his home network.

A moment later, he did a mental conversion of Accelerated World time into real-world time. Graphite Edge had said to change the automatic disconnection safety activation to ten UNF hours later, so the number he should enter into the setting window was a thousandth of ten hours—so then, six hundred minutes equals thirty-six thousand seconds, divided by a thousand—thirty-six seconds...

He managed the calculation in an instant and was about to type the numbers into the screen when a pale hand stretched out abruptly from beside him and grabbed hold of his wrist.

"Fwaah?!" he cried as he looked to his side and found a small face a mere ten centimeters away from his.

Fuko Kurasaki normally wore a gentle smile, but at the moment, her face looked tense somehow, and Haruyuki held his breath. But before he could say anything, Fuko brought her forehead to his and murmured, "Corvus, give me courage."

"Huh?" Haruyuki didn't understand what she meant, but he reflexively squeezed her hand firmly anyway. Instantly, a deep shudder came to him through the parts of their bodies that were

touching. It was only after that that he heard her voice more firmly:

"Thank you. Shall we go?"

"S-sure."

The way Fuko was acting was indeed concerning, but he didn't have the time to be bewildered. With each second that passed on this side, sixteen minutes and forty seconds went by in the Unlimited Neutral Field. Once he finished changing the automatic disconnection settings, they nodded at each other and chanted the command in unison, "Unlimited Burst."

Together with the sound of acceleration, his field of view went dark, and the warmth of Fuko's body disappeared, along with the smell of her shampoo. What he felt in their place was a cloak of cold air and the crisp scent of wood.

When he opened his eyes, head still hanging, the feet of Silver Crow, wrapped in their silver armor, were braced on a white, natural-wood floor. Apparently, the Change had come while they were in the real world.

"A...Heian stage maybe..." He lifted his head and looked around.

Naturally, he was still in the same location as he was before the automatic disconnection, the small room in front of the Shrine of the Eight Divines in the deepest level of the Castle. But he could see only Sky Raker a little ways off; the master-student duo of Graph and Lead were nowhere to be found.

He was curious about where they'd gone, but since Fuko's appearance before they accelerated still bothered him, he walked over to Raker and asked timidly, "Um, Master? Is something the matter?"

Fuko lifted her hanging face mask and shook her head. "I'm sorry for saying something so strange out of the blue like that, Corvus. I was just a little...scared."

"Scared? ...*You*?" Haruyuki was stunned.

"Yes." Fuko nodded, setting her fluid metal hair in motion. "I...I have an obligation to tell Sacchi everything we learn today.

But...what if what Graph tells us is something that will bring her not hope but despair? What if it's something that will crush the desire she's kept with her all this time, for so many years, the yearning to see the end of the Accelerated World? When that thought struck me, I was suddenly seized with fear."

Haruyuki gasped beneath his goggles. The reason he had taken on the challenge of breaking into the Castle again today in secret from Kuroyukihime was to investigate the seventh Arc, The Fluctuating Light. He wanted to get information on it—the item Metatron had declared to be the reason for the existence of Brain Burst—and tell Kuroyukihime about the possibility of another path.

He had simply assumed it was nothing but unexpected good fortune when they ran into not only Trilead Tetroxide but also Graphite Edge after slipping through Suzaku's ferocious attack to arrive in the Castle, because Graph probably had more detailed knowledge than Lead about the Castle—and about Brain Burst itself.

But it was true there were no guarantees that the information Graph disclosed to them would be what Haruyuki had been hoping for. Graph might declare that TFL was not a condition for clearing Brain Burst. Or that even if it was, reaching it was utterly impossible.

Haruyuki shifted his gaze to the far wall. The entrance to the Shrine of the Eight Divines had been a temple-like arch blocked by a silver fence in the Moonlight stage, but now in the Heian stage, it had transformed into crimson *torii* gates closed off by a snowy-white sacred rope. In the deep darkness beyond it, he could see the hazy pulse of the golden light on the pedestal.

It was, at most, only a hundred meters from the sacred rope to the pedestal. But in practical terms, that distance was infinite. He could barely just *evade* Suzaku, a single God, so he was convinced he'd never be able to cross those hundred meters, guarded as they were by eight super-class Enemies with God powers.

Fuko also stared at the golden light from his side. "I wonder what Sacchi would do if she were here, hmm?" she murmured softly.

He thought for a bit and then answered, "Knowing Kuroyukihime, I feel like she would try charging in there to see what would happen."

"You and Pile would do everything in your power to stop her, though." Chuckling, Fuko touched the thick sacred rope and then took a step back. "I'm sorry for my sudden weakness, Corvus. I'm all right now. No matter what Graph tells us, Sacchi would never give up or despair as easily as that. My duty is to cut down any obstacles ahead of her and fly—whatever sky might await us."

"Um." Haruyuki also moved away from the sacred rope and touched her arm gently. "I-I'll fly, too. With you, Master...for Kuroyukihime's sake."

"Thank you, Corvus." Smiling gently, Fuko looked around the small room. "Still...I wonder where Graph and Lead went off to."

"Yeah. We were in the real world for about fifteen seconds, so only a little over four hours should have passed here, but..."

"You've gotten faster at accelerated calculations, hmm?"

He shrank at the unexpected praise and then had a sudden realization. "Oh! R-right. Please wait a moment..." He focused his mind and started to call the master of the underground labyrinth in distant Shiba Park. As the link was established, a 3-D icon terminal appeared on his shoulder and bobbed gently.

"That took quite a lot of time, servant." The Archangel Metatron sounded peeved.

"Sorry." Haruyuki hurried to apologize. "I'm sorry for making you wait, Metatron. And also...do you know where Graph and Lead went?"

"Listen to me, servant. In this state, the instant the link with you is severed, all sensory information is also interrupted. Which is to say, there is no reason why I would know."

"R-right. Hmm...Maybe they went to have dinner or something..." A place on the level of the Castle would maybe have a super-luxurious restaurant-type shop somewhere, he wondered, casting his eyes around the room again.

Then he heard the thunder of one heavy impact after another from high above and looked over at Fuko. She nodded at him, and they started to run. They leapt onto the staircase opposite the sacred rope and raced up the stairs two at a time.

What they saw when they entered the Hall of the Arc half a minute later was the entirely unexpected sight of a gray-armored warrior over four meters tall swinging its sword against a young sky-blue samurai a third its size in the center of the hall. The bigger one was most likely one of the Castle's guard Enemies, while the smaller was without a doubt Trilead Tetroxide.

With his slender straight sword, Lead caught the blade of the warrior Enemy, which looked like it could sever even stone. Snowy-white sparks jetted out from where their blades made contact, illuminating the gloomy hall. Lead had managed to brace himself for the present moment, but the difference in power and weight was clear. At some point, the equilibrium would crumble, and Lead would be struck with a fatal blow.

"Wh-wh-wh—? Sh-sh-sh—," Haruyuki stammered hoarsely. *What is going on?! Should we do something?!*

"Oh!" A black shadow passed by the pedestal where the Arc Destiny had once been safely enshrined. "Rekka! Crow! You're back!"

"This is not a 'you're back' situation, Graph!" Fuko returned sharply, pressing in on the man. "Why is this happening?! You have to hurry and help him!"

"Nah, don't panic." Graph raised his hands to hold her off and continued lazily, "So like, the Change happened while we were waiting for you guys to get back. Both Lead and I haven't had a Heian stage for a while, so I figured we'd double-check the route home and clean up some Enemies while we were at it."

"Then why are you making Trilead do it by himself?!" Fuko scolded. "It's dangerous!"

"It's fine; he's fine. He gets the job done when it needs to be done. I mean, he's my student—," Graph started, but he was interrupted by Lead.

"I-I'm sorry, Master." His voice was pained as he continued to push back against the Enemy blade. "It's getting a little difficult."

"Oh-ho! Well, that is like the third or fourth one. Hmm... Okay then..." Cocking his head slightly to one side, Graphite Edge raised a hand and snapped a finger at Haruyuki. "Sorry, Crow. Get in there and help Trilead."

"Wh-whaaat?! Me?!"

"Yup. Oh, but no Incarnate techniques."

"Um...Okay...But...Uh..." Stunned, he alternated between looking at Graph and Lead, but the situation did not change. In fact, Lead's straight sword was gradually being pushed back. He wouldn't be able to hang on forever.

*I don't even know what's going on, but I have to get in there, I guess!*

He shelved his myriad doubts and took a deep breath before starting to run across the white wood floor. For a fleeting instant, he took some bit of courage from Fuko's cheer of "You can do it, Corvuuuus!" that chased him from behind, but then the cold voice of Metatron echoed in his ear:

"Servant, that Being's weapon has a relatively high priority. Your thin armor will not be able to completely defend against it."

"Ee—"

"Your attack will have to be entirely composed of evasion. Well, if I am so inclined, I shall warn you in advance."

"...P-please do." He groaned in reply and stared straight ahead.

Trilead had his back turned to him, but he had to have noticed Haruyuki's approach. However, it was all he could do to hold off the Enemy's large sword; he couldn't move from that position. Haruyuki had to first strike the Enemy to get it to change targets. Fortunately, his health gauge was in fine condition after he'd spent the ten points to re-log in.

"Lead!!" Haruyuki cried, kicking at the floor to jump. He flew over Trilead from behind, and once he had bounded close to the

Enemy's face, he beat down with a right straight with the whole weight of his body behind it squarely in the center of that terrifying mask. "Un…hyah!"

The feedback was fierce. The still-full health gauge displayed above the warrior's head decreased the slightest amount. This seemed to be the first attack in practical terms, and the burning-red eyes of the warrior latched onto Haruyuki.

"Zoooooowaaaaan!" With a curious battle cry, it brandished its massive sword, at least two meters in length.

Released from its pressure, Trilead nimbly leapt backward, and Haruyuki used the slight charge in his special-attack gauge to deploy the wings on his back.

"Servant, from the right."

The instant after Metatron's voice echoed in his mind, the warrior brought down its massive blade and swung horizontally. Haruyuki had been thinking he would avoid a vertical strike to one side or the other, so if Metatron hadn't warned him, he would have reacted too late.

"Shwah!" With a somewhat pathetic cry, he jumped into the air. The powerful horizontal slash passed directly below his feet, leaving a shimmering mirage in the air.

He got another blow in with his right foot as the Enemy was still swinging its sword, and with the reaction from that, he leapt backward and called out to Trilead as he landed, "It's targeting me now; you watch for openings and attack!"

"Understood, Crow!"

It'd been a while since they'd fought together, but there was no hesitation in Lead's response. The two kicked off the ground simultaneously, and Haruyuki went right while Trilead went left. Just as he'd expected, the Enemy chased after him, whirling its massive body around as it quickly brandished its fat blade.

"A series of attacks is coming, servant!" Metatron said from his shoulder, her voice slightly tense.

Haruyuki kept his field of view—which threatened to contract to the tip of the large blade—wide to take in the whole Enemy and waited.

"Zooooiii!" With a roar, the massive body began to move. From the flow of power and the change in its center of gravity, Haruyuki picked up the trajectory of the sword.

*It's true that one blow is ridiculously powerful...but in terms of technique, it's not as sharp as Manganese Blade!*

*Zmm! Zmm! Zmm!* Three high-speed slashes came one after the other, ripping through the air. Vertical, vertical, horizontal. But Haruyuki managed to evade them all on the order of millimeters. More precisely, the last hack just barely scraped against his chest armor, but he took essentially no damage.

The blue shimmer of a sword flashed suddenly behind the warrior. Lead's slashing attack landed a clean hit in the middle of the Enemy's back and whisked away a significant part of its health gauge. At this decisive display of power, he wanted to make a witty comment about how he'd expect nothing less from the Arc Infinity, but if he didn't do something quick, the warrior's target would shift back to Lead.

"Hyaah!" He dived in close to the warrior and beat at the thin armor of his knee joints with punches and kicks. He shot off five blows in a single breath, but the damage he did didn't begin to compare with Lead's power. Three more hits—no, two...

"Zoaaaam!" The warrior roared and tried to catch Haruyuki with the pommel of the thick blade.

He hurried to duck, but the lump of metal—mass equivalent to a large, blunt weapon—grazed his left shoulder, and just that was enough to bring his health gauge down nearly 10 percent. Haruyuki bounded backward.

"You pushed in too far, servant," Metatron reprimanded him.

"Y-yes, I know. But I have to do more damage..." *Or I won't be able to keep it targeting me*, he was going to say, but the Archangel cut him off with harsh, meaningful words:

"You take a Being as far too logical a presence. Being only

newly born, their powers of thought don't begin to compare with my own, but even so, they possess something that one might call a mind."

"A mind…?!" He was stunned for an instant but then quickly remembered Coolu, the lesser-Enemy of the Lava Carbuncle type. This friend of Petit Paquet had indeed appeared to have something Haruyuki believed was a soul. As he came to this realization, he heard Metatron once more.

"Thus it is not necessarily the case that they will always set their sights on the one who deals them the most damage."

"Huh? So then, what's the standard?"

"I'm telling you, there exists no standard that can clearly be put into numbers. It's the same as with you little warriors. Beings will attack the target they perceive as a threat, and that is not determined on the basis of damage alone."

This conversation—which was actually taking place not with voices but super-high-speed thoughts—sparked a certain memory in Haruyuki. The mission a month earlier to rescue Ardor Maiden from where she was imprisoned at the Castle's south gate. The God Suzaku had turned the brunt of its attack not on Black Lotus, although she was the one dealing it constant damage, but on Silver Crow, who had been flying toward the south gate. At the time, Haruyuki had keenly felt Suzaku's wrath at this little creature trying to penetrate his sacred territory.

Enemies—Beings—were not mere programs. They were sometimes stirred by anger and sometimes made connections with a Burst Linker, just like Chocolat Puppeter and Coolu—or Haruyuki and Metatron. In which case, he had to make this warrior Enemy feel like Haruyuki was more of a threat than Lead.

He couldn't use Incarnate techniques, but he *could* hone his image until he was on the verge of Incarnate—the so-called fighting spirit, to put it neatly. He might not be able to manage the overwhelming aura that gushed from the Black or Red Kings on the battlefield, but he could increase his will to fight, throw away his hesitations, and confront his foe.

Right. At some point, a seed of hesitation had sprouted in him at the idea of fighting Enemies. Maybe because he'd met the "Being" Metatron or because he'd fought to protect Coolu. Or maybe he'd already felt it the first time he saw an Enemy.

He'd tried to actively take part in the hunts to earn points without confessing this to his comrades, but he never could get serious in an Enemy fight the way he did in a fight against another player, probably because the reason for fighting was flimsy. Enemies were frightening and strong, and if you let your guard slip, they'd destroy you. But was it really okay to attack them, creatures under system orders to attack, ordered just to win some points? The thought just wouldn't go away.

As he confronted this warrior Enemy now—which was probably Beast level in status—Haruyuki asked the question he'd wanted to ask for a long time: "Metatron. What do you think of us fighting Beings?"

"That is for you little warriors to decide," the Legend-class Enemy responded immediately, then added after a brief pause, "however, I believe that if the Beings are going to fight you, then that is proof of their existence."

"Proof...of their existence?"

"Yes. Without exception, when we awaken in this world, we know nothing other than fighting you Burst Linkers. However, more than a few Beings find a new reason for existing after surviving numerous fights and continuing to live for eternity. In which case, there is certainly meaning in us fighting. This is what I believe."

*Meaning in fighting.* Haruyuki nodded and stepped firmly onto the floorboards with both feet. A moment later, he raised his hands into position.

It wasn't that he completely understood what Metatron was saying. And it wasn't as though his hesitation about fighting Enemies had vanished. But the warrior Enemy before him was using all his force to try to defeat Haruyuki and Lead. In which case, Haruyuki had to do the same. Even if his opponent was an Enemy, this was a Brain Burst duel, after all.

All thought vanished from his mind as the color palette of the world shifted toward the blue, and he felt the super-acceleration that had come over him any number of times now. But this time, in addition to the change in palette, the Enemy's heavy armor gradually grew translucent.

He could see the particles of light flowing inside the massive body. This was the first time this had happened, but he instinctively understood that the particles were the information that made up the Enemy itself. Most likely, because he had been focusing his mind while communicating with Metatron, his perceptions were in the tiniest bit of alignment with the Highest Level.

The warrior started to turn toward Trilead, but then, as if sensing something, it looked at Haruyuki. In the depths of its mask, the fires of its eyes blazed red. The warrior raised a foot where particles of light were gathering.

"Zrrraaaaaah!!"

The instant the Enemy launched a stomp attack, Haruyuki jumped.

The warrior's foot hit the floorboards hard, while the gathering light—its power made visible—dispersed in concentric waves. If he'd stayed on the floor, he might have been caught up in the shock wave and knocked over. But he evaded that fate with room to spare and used the warrior's extended knee as a stepping stone for a two-tiered jump. He got in another clean hit, a fist in the face, likely its weak point.

From there, Haruyuki moved with dizzying speed to keep the warrior's focus firmly on himself, while Lead beat down with all his might, darting in with a slashing attack as the openings presented themselves.

The battle seemed both infinite and fleeting until finally the warrior's massive bulk exploded and scattered, leaving behind one final thunderous roar. An instant later, Haruyuki dropped out of his super-accelerated state. He staggered, dizzy, and nearly fell—only to be caught by Lead's firm hand.

"Are you all right, Crow?"

"Y-yeah," Haruyuki somehow managed. "I just got a little dizzy there."

"I'm sorry," Lead said apologetically. "I left you to be the target the whole time."

Haruyuki glanced at his face mask, and a laugh slipped out of him.

"Wh-what's the matter?"

"Ha-ha! Sorry. I'm sorry. It's just you using net game words like *target*."

The young warrior shrugged, somewhat embarrassed. "When I'm with Master Graph, I accidentally start talking like him."

"Nah, I think it's great. I can get on board with that, too," he replied, pulling himself upright when he heard a two-person applause from the rear.

"Pretty good fighting style there, my students. There's really nothing left for me to teach—," Graphite Edge started, somewhat theatrically, and Sky Raker shoved a sharp elbow into his side.

"Hold on, Graph. Corvus is *my* student."

"Urgh," the swordmaster groaned. "It doesn't matter, though, right? And if I teach him just one thing, then he's my student, too, after all."

"Are you saying you taught him something?" Raker demanded.

"Huh." Graph scratched his helmet. "Maybe nothing yet?"

The absurd conversation brought wry smiles to the faces of the younger Burst Linkers, and Haruyuki glanced backward. He closed his eyes briefly at the traces of the fierce battle carved into the wooden floor.

"The soul of that Being has returned to the Main Visualizer and will be reborn someday in a new form to perhaps fight you again," Metatron murmured from his shoulder.

"Yeah, I guess so." He joined Lead and returned to where Fuko and Graph stood.

The young samurai bowed to his master, and although he showed only the slightest sign of fatigue, his voice was crisp and clear as always. "Master Graph, thank you for your instruction."

"Yup. Nice work. You're really getting the hang of that thing, Lead." Graph pointed to the Arc Infinity, and Lead glanced down at his left hip before shaking his head.

"No. I'm still nowhere near your level, Master. When the battle drags on, I feel the weight of this sword."

"Well, of course you do," Graph said. "I mean, it *is* a mighty Arc, after all. There aren't too many swords in this whole Accelerated World heavier than that one."

"Huh. Is it really that heavy?" Haruyuki asked, distracted.

Lead cocked his head slightly to one side. "Would you like to hold it, Crow?" He had no sooner asked than, without waiting for an answer, he was removing it from the sheath on his hip. "Go ahead."

Lead held the straight sword up in both hands, and Haruyuki looked at his face, then Graph's, then Raker's, but everyone seemed fine with the idea. He swallowed hard before he timidly raised his hands.

"O-okay then, if you don't mind— Wh-whoa!!" The instant he took the sword from Lead's hands, Haruyuki very nearly dropped it and hurriedly braced himself. It was indeed heavy. He had only the memory to compare to now, but it might have been as heavy as the great sword Chrome Disaster had been equipped with, if not heavier. "Y-you were swinging *this* thing around…? Um. C-can I take it out of the sheath?"

"Please, go ahead," Lead acquiesced with a smile, so Haruyuki carefully gripped the hilt and drew the sword.

When he looked at the blade of The Infinity up close for the first time, he noticed that it shone crisp and cool like ice, the straight lines of the tempering rising up in the bluish steel. Haruyuki had mainly fought with a sword when he was the Sixth Disaster, but when he felt again the weight and danger of the sword as an Enhanced Armament, he could see it would be no easy task to master it.

"Hmm. It has a fairly high priority," Metatron said, flapping her wings with deep interest. "Servant, hit it with Ektenia."

"N-n-n-n-no way! I can't pay for it if I break it!" He hurriedly re-sheathed the sword and handed it back to Lead. He waited until the young samurai had hung it from his left hip again and then let out a deep breath. "It's only natural you'd get tired, fighting with such a heavy weapon."

"No." Lead shook his head firmly. "If I'm feeling the weight of the sword after a mere three battles, it simply means that I still have a long way to go."

"B-but," Haruyuki protested, "I mean, when I get tired, I feel even the weight of my own arms and legs."

"It doesn't look that way at all, Crow. The way you moved in the battle earlier..." Lead paused. "It was so smooth that I was vaguely fearful."

"Huh? Oh, th-th-th-that was..." Now it was Haruyuki's turn to shake his head.

However, Graph nodded solemnly, "I had the same thought in that mock battle the other day when you had that exchange with G. Your physical techniques, Crow—the way you fight at super-close range in three dimensions at top speed is already high-ranker territory. I guess Rekka and Lota gave good instruction."

"Naturally." Fuko sniffed. "Of course, there was also Corvus's own hard work."

"N-n-n-n-n-no-no-no, not at all." Haruyuki, unused to praise, could only shake his head even faster from side to side. "I mean, with the Green King—and the Enemy just now—I could barely do any damage or anything."

"Right. Right there." Graph snapped a finger at him. "Fighting-type duel avatars like you who have no Enhanced Armament can master how to use their bodies faster than other types...sometimes. That's the foundation of the duel, a critically important skill. But when you go up levels, it stops winning out over those with Enhanced Armament in terms of simple attack power. Meaning that when your opponent's hard like G or that warrior Enemy, whether your punches are powerful enough to break the enemy's defenses also comes into play...Oh! When

I say powerful here, I don't mean the physical power of the punch."

"We understand that much at least, Graph." Fuko shut the avatar down and immediately picked up where he left off: "I'm also a fighting type with no sword or gun, but to compensate for my relative lack of attack power when fighting an opponent with firm defenses, I use the propulsive power of Gale Thruster and penetrating blows. Corvus has poured his level-up bonuses into enhancing his flight ability, so his flight speed and continuous travel distance are quite good, but his instantaneous thrust doesn't match that of a booster, and he has no special striking abilities."

"Right..." Left with no choice but to agree with this assessment, Haruyuki hung his head. In the fight just now, if Lead hadn't hit the Enemy with such accurate damage, Haruyuki's powers of concentration would have eventually been exhausted, and he would've taken a direct hit from that massive blade.

"But still, you know, the duel can't be won just by guarding. Fighting types with solid moves, sword wielders with powerful swords, heavyweight types with strong defenses—one of the fun parts of Brain Burst is how everyone has these strong points and shortcomings. Put ten Burst Linkers together and you got ten ways of being right," Graphite Edge summed up. He grinned as he added, "But of course, that begs the question of just how scary dangerous Lota is as a *sword-bearing, fighting type.*

"Either way, Crow, no need to get so glum as all that. You totally got what your role was in the impromptu tag match with Lead, and you kept that powerful opponent focused on you right up to the end. From my point of view, you did pretty great for yourself out there. And well, if you're not satisfied with how you are now, you can just get stronger with more training or level-up bonuses or whatever. And if you come across an opponent you can't beat even then—"

"If you can't beat them alone, then you can beat them with two people, and if you can't win with two, you can with three,

Corvus. You have plenty of comrades you can turn to." Fuko beat Graph to the punch, and he scratched his helmet, seeming dissatisfied, while Lead chuckled.

"Yes." Metatron flapped up above his head. "And of course, you can also turn to me, your master!"

To let Trilead—exhausted after three spontaneous Enemy battles in a row—rest, the party moved once more to the secure basement. The instant they sat down in a circle on the wooden floor, the young samurai let out a long, thin sigh. Haruyuki felt like there was no need to sit formally at a time like this at least, but when he saw Trilead's upright bearing even as tired as he was, he couldn't actually say that. And anyway, no matter how many hours they sat formally on their knees, a duel avatar's knees didn't get tired, and their feet didn't fall asleep—supposedly.

"It's too bad there's no tea and snacks," Fuko commented.

"Well, if you're looking for a shop, there *is* one in the Castle." Graph shrugged. "But the location's totally random. It's basically a hidden room, so consider yourself super-lucky if you do come across it."

"Ohh." Fuko nodded. "Does that mean they sell good things there?"

"Well, it *is* the hidden shop of the final dungeon. I've found it a couple times, and the first time, I nearly threw all the points I had at them— No, I mean." The man, sitting lazily cross-legged in contrast with Lead, coughed a little and cleared his throat before sitting up a bit straighter. "At any rate, Rekka, Crow, thanks for logging in again. Did you change the automatic disconnect time?"

"Yes. To ten hours from now," Haruyuki replied.

"Good." Graph nodded, satisfied, before continuing. "Now we'll have a while to talk. That said, I feel like I told you the important stuff before the disconnect."

"What are you talking about? You still haven't told us anything." Fuko, sitting formally on her knees, sounded exasperated.

"Right before Corvus and I disconnected, you said that this Brain Burst 2039 was a game and also wasn't a game. What does that mean?"

"Ohh. Um, the thing about that." Graph turned his face mask upward like he was looking for the right words but eventually glanced over to the left—toward the depths of the Shrine of the Eight Divines, separated from them by the white sacred rope. Haruyuki followed suit to look that way, too, and the pulsing golden light in the distant darkness came into view.

"Okay, this'll be a little bit of a long story, but I'll tell you what I know." With that preamble, the dual swordsman, Graphite Edge, aka the Anomaly, started to speak slowly, telling his story as though it were a fairy tale.

*A long, long time ago, there was a large battle in a world that closely resembled this one, a battle brought about by a certain "presence" locked away in that world—to borrow Metatron's wording, a Being. The war that waged between the two sides was long and fierce. Although the world was virtual, much blood was spilled, and many lives were lost from that world.*

*The objective of one side was the destruction of the Being in question. The objective of the other side was to free the Being from the world. After years of fighting, the leaders of the two sides discovered at basically the same time a console that would allow them to exercise administrator privileges in this virtual world—game master privileges. But that was all the console gave them, so the only thing they could do was generate and place objects and monsters within the already maximum resource range; the console didn't allow soldiers on either side—players—to directly annihilate the other or the Being at the heart of the matter.*

*So the leader whose aim was to destroy the Being—let's call him A. As an alternative plan, he tried to lock the Being away in the virtual world forever. He created an enormous dungeon at the center of the world, sealed the Being in the deepest level, and had the area guarded by eight of the most powerful class of monsters. Moreover,*

*he made the dungeon itself an impregnable, impenetrable strong-hold protected by four similarly powerful monsters.*

*Meanwhile, the other leader, B, whose start had been delayed only a few minutes, challenged A to a fight and won. But by that time, A had completely locked the stronghold, and B could not rescue the Being with GM privileges. Leader B and the players they commanded were forced to attack the stronghold under their own power. But the four guard monsters A had placed there were overwhelmingly—no, hopelessly strong, and B and their army could not defeat even one of them. B's comrades fell one after another, and finally, B, too, had to abandon the attack.*

*So they decided to entrust their hope to the future. To believe that at some point, warriors powerful enough to defeat the four gatekeeper monsters would come, penetrate the stronghold, take down the eight guardian monsters, and release the Being.*

Even after Graphite Edge closed his mouth, no one said anything for a while. It was too abstract a story, the details too difficult to visualize. It seemed to Haruyuki that a war in a virtual world that worked on a game program was, when it came down to it, simply a multiplayer fighting game, but Graph sounded like he was recounting a real war.

Still, there were a few things he could imagine. After exchanging a look with Fuko, Haruyuki began timidly, "Um. So the stronghold in your story's the Castle, the four gatekeeper monsters are the Four Gods, the sealed Being is the last Arc, The Fluctuating Light... Is that what that's supposed to mean?"

"Well, that's basically the gist of it." Graph nodded.

"So then that means, um, the person who created the Castle and the person who created the rest of the field and the other dungeons are not the same?" Haruyuki asked further. "Is that the cause of the contradiction I felt?"

"Well, that's basically the gist of it." Once again, the double swordmaster nodded.

Indeed, if there were these two leaders—A, the creator of a Castle he didn't want attacked; and B, the creator who wanted to attack it—then that would explain Haruyuki's doubt about whether the creator of Brain Burst wanted the Castle attacked or not. But still, wasn't B taking the long way around here?

"Hmm. So then with the GM privileges, creator B can manipulate every place other than the Castle, right? In that case, couldn't they have just created a ton of Enemies as strong as the Four Gods and had them attack the Castle...or made their own status more powerful than the Four Gods and charged the gates?" Haruyuki wondered.

"First of all," Graph said, raising a finger, "as a general rule, the only ones who can attack monsters are players. You can't manipulate a large army of monsters or make other players bend to your will. It might be possible to control a scant few with special methods, but they'd never win against the Four Gods like that."

Haruyuki worried about Metatron's reaction to this, knowing that she had been tamed with the power of an Enhanced Armament once, so he looked to his shoulder, but the 3-D icon held her silence. When he turned to face forward again, Graph added a second finger.

"Second, there are ways to strengthen players, but those have limits, too. Listen. Creator A placed the most powerful monsters the program would allow—Enemies, in other words, as the Castle gatekeepers. So all the players—the Burst Linkers—can do is also get as strong as the maximum status allowed by the program."

"And that maximum is level ten...is that it?" Fuko asked.

Graph didn't respond right away. Sitting cross-legged still, he crossed his arms and leaned forward. "Hmm. The thing is...I'm thinking maybe the real limit program-wise is level nine."

"What do you mean?" Fuko pressed.

"Mm, it's hard to explain." The avatar's hands rounded as though he were holding a ball. "There's an upper limit to the amount of Burst Points you can earn, too. So Burst Linkers can't keep getting more of them forever, and not every Burst Linker who exists now can become a high ranker. So maybe level nine's the highest level you can reach normally, by spending points and leveling up, and that's related to that resource upper limit. But…Even if you make it to level nine, there's absolutely no way you can defeat the Four Gods. About all you can do is use every Incarnate technique in the book and somehow make it so that can't act temporarily."

Haruyuki remembered when he'd fought Suzaku with Kuroyuki-hime and Fuko. They hadn't been able to defeat it even by dragging it up into the stratosphere, which made Suzaku's flames die out, and beating on it with the full force of the Black King's second-level Incarnate technique Starburst Stream.

"It's true." Perhaps reliving the same memory, Fuko shuddered slightly as she spoke. "I don't feel at all that I'd be able to defeat a God if I went up another level. So then…level ten goes beyond the system limits to fight the Four Gods?"

"Dunno. What I know's limited info from the past; I can only guess from that about the current Accelerated World. But the sudden-death rule—if a level niner loses to another level niner, it's immediate total point loss, and if you get five people down to zero like this, you can get to level ten. For a game, it's abnormally harsh. It wouldn't be at all strange if it was a rule to give you the power to surpass system-wise limits…Or it's testing us," Graphite Edge muttered, half to himself, and then lifted his face as if he'd abruptly realized something and looked at Haruyuki. "Crow, your face says there's a whole lot you can't accept here."

Reflexively, Haruyuki touched his face with both hands. Silver Crow's face mask was covered by mirrored goggles, which were absolutely impossible to see through, and yet, Graph had somehow sensed his expression. He nodded his head up and down.

"Yes. The way you're talking, it sounds like it's not the duel that's the main objective of Brain Burst, but Enemy hunting..."

"Yeah, I guess," Graph agreed. "But that's the way it is. The reason Burst Linkers exist isn't to win against other Burst Linkers, but to reach TFL sealed in the center of the Castle...and that means defeating the Four Gods and the Eight Divines, the strongest of the Enemies."

"So then why is Brain Burst a one-on-one fighting game?!" he shouted, clenching his hands into fists.

"No idea." Graph only shrugged lightly. "In order to attack—no, have the Castle attacked, creator B tried three approaches. Trial one aka Accel Assault, trial two aka Brain Burst, and trial three, Cosmos Corrupt. Apparently, AA was a high-speed shooter with player fights as the main deal; CC was hack and slash with Enemy fights as the main thing. If the objective of all three games was to liberate The Fluctuating Light, then CC would seem to be the closest to that objective. But AA and CC are both long closed down, and all that's left is BB. And I don't think that's mere coincidence. Even setting aside G's hard work."

"Excess fighting...and excess harmony," Fuko remarked. "That's why the worlds of AA and CC fell. According to the White King, at least."

Graph snorted. "Ninety percent of what *she* says is to manipulate other people. You can't take it seriously. Anyway, now I've told you everything I know about The Fluctuating Light. You two be the ones to tell Lota."

The man moved to stand, but Fuko called to him sharply.

"Wait. We still haven't heard the most important part. At the end of the day, what *is* The Fluctuating Light? It's not simply an in-game item. What did you mean by *Being* before?"

"Unfortunately, I don't know that either," Graph said, spreading his hands. "I mean, it's not like I was *there* for this virtual war way back when...You want anything more than that, your only choice is to achieve level ten and ask the developer."

Then where exactly had Graph heard the story he told them? The doubt rose up in Haruyuki's heart, but he felt like he wouldn't get an answer even if he asked the question.

"Um, can I ask just one last thing?" Haruyuki followed Graph to his feet and cast a glance into the darkness beyond the sacred rope before looking at Graph again.

"Yeah. If it's something I can answer."

"Even a guess would be great. If someone does break into the Shrine of the Eight Divines, reach The Fluctuating Light, and remove the seal...what will happen to Brain Burst?"

Graph paused briefly. "Sorry. My only answer to that is 'no idea.' ...But if there was one thing I *could* say...I think the outcome will change the world."

"Change...the world?" Haruyuki parroted. "Do you mean it would bring about a large change in the Accelerated World?"

"No, that's not it." An air of a grin and a daring laugh bled through Graph's face mask. "The real world. Somewhere inside that light is a blow powerful enough to change our lives in the real...That's what I think." He stared at the golden light shimmering in the distant dark.

Haruyuki, Fuko, Lead, and Metatron also stared wordlessly at the final Arc for a while. At the light that was quietly and yet definitely breathing. It really didn't seem like any ordinary item. It called out with a voice that did not form words, as a presence with some kind of will.

"If..." Unconsciously, Haruyuki started to ask the swordsman. "If all of us here now took on the challenge, could we reach that light?"

"No way." The reply came back to him instantly.

Only two words, but their simplicity held an incredible weight.

Haruyuki slowly nodded and closed his eyes. *Right now, there's something else we have to do. When it's time to fight toward that light, I'll come back here again with Kuroyukihime.* Carving this resolve deep into his heart, he lifted his head. What he had gained by coming that day was great. That would have to be enough for now.

"Wohkay." Graph's lazy voice broke the silence. "Sorry for the wait, Lead. You're in charge from here on out...Good luck."

Lead nodded silently, and Haruyuki blinked in surprise.

"Wh-what do you...?"

"It's obvious." The black-clad swordsman thrust out a finger as he smoothly made his announcement: "Lead's leaving this Castle...together with all of you."

# 6

"All right then, Master. Thank you so much again today." Haruyuki bowed his head after walking her to the doorway, and Fuko shook hers with a laugh.

"No, it was a good experience for me, too. I should thank you for bringing me along, Corvus." She slipped on her shoes to the faint sound of motors whirring and set her hand on the door handle. But then she let go and turned back with a serious look. "It's just...I think it's going to take me a little time to process what we learned today. Corvus. When are you going to tell Sacchi?"

"Oh. Right." He paused. "I was thinking today if I could..."

"Were you...? Well, yes, that's fine. All right, I'm sorry, but do you mind if I leave you the job of telling her first?"

"No, of course not." Haruyuki shook his head slightly.

"All right." Now Fuko did actually push the door open. She bowed lightly with the twilight-colored sky behind her. "I'll be on my way then. Have a good evening."

"Thank you. You too!"

She waved with a smile, and once she had disappeared beyond the door, Haruyuki let out a small sigh.

The time was 5:25 PM. It hadn't yet been half an hour since they'd dived into the Unlimited Neutral Field. But in Haruyuki's subjective reality, he had been over there for more than ten hours, so he had ten hours' worth of exhaustion. With the round trip, it had been quite an adventure, slipping past the fierce attacks of the God Suzaku not once but twice.

After he returned to the living room and cleared away their glasses, he flopped down on the sofa and sank back.

"Aaaah," he groaned. "I feel like Suzaku's initial Hate is gradually increasing." He raised one hand to count on his fingers. The first time he encountered Suzaku had been a month earlier, on the outward journey of the mission to rescue Ardor Maiden. With the trip back after that and then that day's return trip, that made four times he had charged across the large bridge to the south, and he keenly felt each time the growth of the God's rage.

And the escape that day—his fourth—was a terrific battle on par with his second close call with Suzaku. They had flown out of the south gate with Lead wedged in between Haruyuki and Fuko, but even still, Suzaku's manifestation was a beat faster, and the three of them had just barely made it out, using Incarnate techniques to defend desperately against the inferno Suzaku rained upon them from overhead.

If they hadn't had Lead's defensive Incarnate technique Genuine Specular, which turned his sword, when brandished horizontally, into a large mirror shield, and the support of Graph's dual swords striking at random with Vorpal Strike from inside the south gate, it would have been utterly impossible to break through. Right from the start, Lead had said escape was impossible without the flight speed of Silver Crow and Sky Raker, and when they managed somehow to flee to Sakurada Street, all three of their health gauges were colored bright red. If they tried that mad dash one more time, it was entirely possibly they'd be wiped out.

"The fifth time, we're gonna have to actually fight and not just sneak past," he muttered to himself, before sitting up and switching mental gears with an "Okay!"

He had taken Fuko on the sudden mission to the Castle and exposed them both to serious danger, but they'd obtained information that was plenty worth it: the origin of the Accelerated

World and the reason for the existence of The Fluctuating Light. And one more thing—an unexpected, trustworthy ally.

*Thanks, Lead...and Graph.* He dipped his head to the east and then stood up. First, he had to get in touch with Kuroyukihime and tell her everything they'd found out. He did some flicking on his virtual desktop, until— "Whoa?!"

Suddenly, the incoming mail icon flashed before his eyes, and he fell back onto the sofa in surprise. He hurried to open it; the body of the message had only the four words: "Arrival in thirty seconds!" And before he could check the sender's name, the door chime sounded, announcing a visitor.

"......"

With a strange look, Haruyuki hurried to the entryway where he had only just seen Fuko off a few minutes ago.

"'Suuuuup!" A red shadow jumped inside and slammed a fist into his side.

"Hrngh!" he groaned. "Wh-what's with the sudden jab?"

"A friendly greeting aaaand angry-sad punishment!" a girl in a red T-shirt and shorts shouted. This was the head of the Legion Prominence, the Red King, Scarlet Rain, aka Yuniko Kozuki.

"Angry-sad?" he asked, stepping back.

"Yup." Niko glared at him, striking a daunting pose on the step into the condo. "You didn't take me to Shibuya on Sunday or anything."

"W-we had the negotiations with Great Wall," he protested.

"And you took *forever* to tell us the results," she sniffed.

"A-a bunch of stuff happened..."

"Welp, suck it up. That's what that gut punch was for." A grin broke through her sullen expression, and a slender figure appeared in the half-open door.

"Hi," said Blood Leopard aka Pard, dressed in riding leather.

"Hello, Pard." He bowed lightly. "What's up all of a sudden?"

"SRY. We have something urgent to talk about."

"Yup. I'm coming iiiin!" Niko walked into the living room, overly familiar with the house, and Haruyuki hurried after her.

He sat them on the sofa, poured cold tea in the glasses he'd just washed, and brought them out to the living room again. He took a sip of his own tea to calm himself down before turning to Niko, who was now sitting directly across from him. "So. What did you want to talk about?"

"Ohh, about that..." Perhaps thirsty, Niko drank down the cold-brew green tea in a single go and turned a slender finger toward the floor of the living room. "You're not calling Kuroyukihime over?"

"Huh? Kuroyukihime?" It was an unexpected demand, but Haruyuki had been about to get in touch with her anyway. "Um. Okay, I'll just send her a mail."

He launched the mailer he had been about to start up before the two girls arrived and quickly sent her a message; the response came right away. It seemed that Kuroyukihime had just left school. She would be there in ten minutes.

The chime rang eight minutes later, in fact.

A uniformed Kuroyukihime followed him into the living room. "Oh-ho?" she said, the moment she caught sight of Niko and Pard on the sofa, her voice containing all kinds of nuance. Her gaze shifted to Haruyuki, and a smile of ultimate chill—well, not that far, a *coolish* smile rose up on her face. "Haruyuki, mind telling me what the situation here is?"

"O-oh! Um! ...Oh! M-Master Fuko was here before, but—!"

"Oh-ho-*ho*?"

"Uh! Um! But I guess Niko and Pard are here for something else...!"

"Oh-ho-ho-*ho*?" Kuroyukihime's smile grew increasingly broad.

"Hey, Black," came a voice from the sofa. "C'mon, sit."

"This isn't your house, Red!" Kuroyukihime whirled around to shout before stepping over briskly and throwing herself down next to Niko.

Secretly letting out a sigh of relief, Haruyuki moved to the kitchen and got another glass, a bottle of cold tea, and a large plate of biscuits before returning to the living room. He poured tea for Kuroyukihime and refills for Niko and Pard and then sat down himself on the sofa.

"Um, Kuroyukihime, I'm really sorry for asking you over all of a sudden," Haruyuki apologized once more.

"No." Kuroyukihime finally let him see her usual smile. "I have some things I'd like to discuss as well. But first and foremost, I shall hear what Niko's business is. What exactly did you want to talk about?"

"Ohh." Niko had just bitten into a caramel-banana cookie, so she wet her mouth with tea before saying with excessive nonchalance, "So like, actually, I was thinking we'd merge Promi with Negabu."

"......"

Haruyuki and Kuroyukihime were struck dumb for a full five seconds at least before they both threw their heads back in shock.

"S-sorryyyyyy?!" she shrieked.

"Whaaaaaaat?!" he yelped.

Five minutes later:

After listening to Niko's explanation with additional commentary from Pard, Kuroyukihime silently ate a cinnamon-almond cookie before saying "I see."

"Huh?" Haruyuki asked. "Um. Is that all, Kuroyukihime?"

"Mmm." She nodded. "What do you think, Haruyuki?"

"O-oh, it's totally nothing like that, but…I don't know. This is too big. What am I supposed to think all of a sudden…? And like in front of me…" He turned his head and asked Niko, "Are you really sure? If you merge with Nega Nebulus, the Legions of the other Kings are going to be even more hostile."

"I already talked about all of that with Pard. I've made my decision." She glanced at the young woman in question before continuing. "I want to fight the Acceleration Research Society…and the White Legion, and the only way to do that is in the Territories with Negabu—But, bah…It's not really a system-wise reason like that. I just wanna fight together. Thinking about it, the first time I fought with you guys six months ago, with the whole fifth Chrome Disaster thing, it was 'cause of the Society, too. I wanna see this fight with them to the end. Otherwise, neither my Legion members nor I will be able to move forward." Her words contained equal parts Niko-like fire and a coolness that reflected her growth.

Kuroyukihime closed her eyes briefly and then slowly nodded. "Ever since I heard that you were thinking about coming to Umesato Junior High, I've anticipated that this might be a possible future. But…this decision came sooner than I expected. To be honest, you've surprised me."

"I-it's not like I said I was gonna go to Umesato 'cause I wanted to merge our Legions or anything," Niko replied quickly, seeming slightly embarrassed. "That's that; this is this."

"Yes. I know." Kuroyukihime suddenly turned a faint smile on her. "At any rate, I must respond to your resolve properly…" She turned her whole body to the left and snapped to attention.

"Niko—no, leader of Prominence, Scarlet Rain," she began, her voice clear. "As Black Lotus, leader of Nega Nebulus, I shall accept your request to merge Legions. I would like to bring in the executives of both sides to discuss at a later date the conditions for the merger. I look forward to fighting alongside you from now on." She offered her hand in a supple motion.

Niko opened her eyes wide for a mere instant and then slapped her hand against Kuroyukihime's to shake it so forcefully it made a snapping noise. "Us, too," she replied, her own voice equally resolute. "Looking forward to it."

The moment he saw their two hands tightly joined, Haruyuki felt something hot welling up from deep in his chest, and he hurriedly blinked it away.

A Legion merger sounded like quite a big deal, but Nega Nebulus and Prominence had already had a peace treaty for some time now. He couldn't count the number of times he'd fought with Niko and Pard, and maybe this was just one step forward in their cooperation. At any rate, what he could say for sure was that this merger wouldn't have happened were it not for the presence of a

common enemy, the Acceleration Research Society. But still, in this moment, a definite miracle took shape.

Kuroyukihime had once assessed her duel avatar as the ultimate in ugly. She'd said that she didn't even have hands to clasp with anyone. Niko had in the past declared her own duel avatar to be like the spines on a hedgehog, that it was her longing to keep the world at bay given material form. They'd quarreled plenty, built up a sort of friendship and trust, and now here they were, finally joining hands.

*I will definitely never forget this sight. No matter what happens to the Legion—or the Accelerated World or Brain Burst itself.*

Resolving this in his heart, Haruyuki blinked firmly one last time and then looked over to Pard, at his right. There, he witnessed the ever-cool Bloody Kitty secretly wiping tears from the corners of her eyes, and his mouth softened.

But noticing the look on Haruyuki's face, Pard returned a slight glare.

"Oh, I'll say this just in case, Niko. Even when our Legions become one, Haruyuki is *my* child and student. Ensure that you do not push your way into his home so casually."

"Huh? Huuuuh?!" Niko shouted, shaking Kuroyukihime's hand away. "This is Negabu's Mission Control center, yeah? But like, once we merge, it's my Mission Control, too, y'know? That's actually like an 'anytime free pass.'"

"D-don't be ridiculous! Use is off-limits unless you get my permission in advance!"

*Um, this is my house, though…*All Haruyuki could do was gape, the words lodged in his throat.


The detailed negotiations involving the executive members of both Legions were set for the next day, July 19, a Friday evening, while the merger ceremony and the meet and greet for all Legion members were decided for the twentieth, Saturday afternoon—immediately before the Territories. And that was the end of the merger talk for the time being.

The Territories in two days' time would also be the decisive battle with the White Legion, so the process was a bit rushed. But they had to avoid at all costs any leak of the attack mission on Minato Area No. 3 to the Oscillatory side. They didn't particularly expect there would be a leak from Prominence, but simply because that Legion was overwhelming in number, Niko proposed that the announcement to all members should be made immediately before the mission.

However, on the other hand, this meant they couldn't really have anyone from Prominence on the Minato No. 3 attack team. Naturally, Niko, who was level nine like Kuroyukihime, couldn't take part, so the support from Prominence would likely be two or three members including Pard.

Of course, this was a big ask, and they were grateful to have the assistance of Prominence members in the defense of Suginami area. But the issue of insufficient personnel on the attack team was still not resolved. Even at a bare minimum, the estimate was that there would be twelve people on the Oscillatory defense team, and at maximum, there could be as many as twenty. Meanwhile, adding in the help from Prominence to leader Fuko and members Utai, Akira, Takumu, Chiyuri, and Haruyuki, the attack team would still only be nine people. If push came to shove, they could have the three former members of Petit Paquet join in, but then only Kuroyukihime would be left for the defense of Suginami, and that was just a bit worrisome.

*We really do need three more people. But I don't have any idea of who else to ask*, Haruyuki muttered to himself, counting the number of people on his fingers, and then suddenly remembered his great adventure of an hour or so earlier and clenched his hand into a fist.

*No, I might be able to wrangle one person, though. But I have to wait for him to contact me…If he'd join us, I'd feel a million times more confident.*

"...yuki. Haruyuki."

He suddenly realized he was being called and hurried to lift his face. "Oh! Y-yes! How about some more cookies?!"

"I hope that I'm not that much of a glutton." Kuroyukihime gave a smile and checked Haruyuki as he was about to leap to his feet with the wave of a hand. "That reminds me. You said earlier that Fuko was here? What did she want?"

"Oh...Th-that's right. I wanted to talk to you about that..." He got that far and then shifted his gaze to the right.

He met the eyes of Niko as she bit into a macadamia-chocolate cookie and Pard while she chewed a coconut-lemon one. He screwed up his face unconsciously as he thought.

*Is it okay to tell them everything Graphite Edge told us? No, that's not a problem. I mean, they're going to be my comrades in the same Legion and all...And we did fight the God Seiryu together...*

"You're making a weird face," Niko remarked. "Did you want my half-eaten cookie?"

"N-n-n-no!" He hurriedly rejected her offer and cleared his throat. "Um, the truth is...Today I kinda went to the Castle..."

"Wh-what?!" Kuroyukihime screeched.

"Th-the Castle?!" Niko howled.

"OMG," Pard muttered.

By the time Haruyuki finished telling them the secrets of the Accelerated World he had saved in his analogue memory, it was 6:40 PM. The southern sky was violet, and the evening sun, on the verge of setting, created a powerful contrast in the room. The western light reflected off the flooring to be absorbed into the girls' eyes, making them shine like jewels.

Or perhaps this glittering light was coming from inside them. Even after Haruyuki closed his mouth, they stayed silent for a long time, but he could sense that each of them was chasing down powerful thoughts at top speed.

When the in-ceiling air conditioner started automatically, filling the air with the faint whir of operation, Kuroyukihime shuddered. She lifted her lowered eyes and looked directly at him. Her lips moved slightly two or three times until finally he heard a faint voice. "The Fluctuating Light..."

She let out a long sigh and then raised her voice slightly. "Let me say this first, Haruyuki."

"O-okay." Haruyuki unconsciously sat up straighter.

"Thank you." Kuroyukihime dipped her head toward him. "You took a terrible risk for my sake...But next time, make sure you say something in advance. I can't even count how many times you've gone off recklessly like this."

Haruyuki bobbed his head up and down at this heartfelt thank-you and minor scolding.

Kuroyukihime's mouth relaxed into a small smile, but she quickly recomposed herself and said in a severe voice, "Youkou, the final Arc. So Graphite Edge said...reaching it is the final objective in Brain Burst. It is the reason for our existence as Burst Linkers."

"Yes. No mistake," he confirmed.

"I see. In other words, that mission to attack the Castle that destroyed the former Nega Nebulus...We were not incorrect in our aim then..." Kuroyukihime leaned back against the sofa and looked up at the evening sky beyond the window with narrowed eyes.

Silence fell once more, and this time, it was Pard who opened her mouth. "Two...developers."

"Mmm," Niko groaned. "So the whosit who made the Castle and the one who designed all the other elements are two different people. So that's why that stupid palace totally rejects us then..."

"Yeah," Haruyuki agreed. "But Castle creator A was defeated by creator B. That's what Graph said, so I think in practical terms, the Brain Burst developer is B alone now..."

The furrow between Niko's brows became that much deeper. "That 'defeated' is a pretty vague way of putting it. This war way back in the long ago happened in a virtual world, yeah? So then didn't A just run out of HP and log out? ...Did they lose their memory, too, like with Brain Burst? Or did they really die in the real world?"

Niko's questions were right on the money, but all Haruyuki could do was shrug helplessly. "Aah. Uh, I didn't ask about that."

"And what's this war in a virtual world anyway? And what exactly is this 'Being' they were fighting over?"

"Oh…Sorry, I don't really…"

"Gah! This is so annoying!" At some point, Niko had taken off her socks, and now she kicked her skinny legs as she shouted, "Hey, Haruyuki, get Graphite Edge over here pronto!"

"I—I can't! I don't know how to contact him or anything…"

"Huh?!" she shrieked in disbelief. "He used to be one of Negabu's Four Elements, yeah?! You didn't even exchange mail addresses?!"

"Oh! No! I told him mine," Haruyuki replied quickly. "But he didn't tell me his…"

"Ngaaah! I'll never be able to make my new Legion thing work like this!"

Her frustrated kicking in the air grew fiercer, and Kuroyukihime, who had been in silent thought, yanked on one of her pigtails.

"Hey!" she snapped. "I can't just let that 'my new Legion' thing slide, you know."

"That doesn't matter right now! Just let it go!" Niko howled, but it seemed that she had succeeded in cooling down at last. She let out a long sigh as she clasped her hands behind her head and looked up at the ceiling.

"Mmm. Hmmm. It's like I get ten answers, and my questions multiply by a hundred or something. So like…to start with, that Graphite Edge, how's he know all this stuff?"

Haruyuki didn't have the words to answer this question, either. He turned his gaze toward Kuroyukihime, and a knowing grin came across the lips of Graph's student.

"Apologies, but I know very little about him myself," she said. "We've never met in the real, either. All that's certain is that he's an Originator."

"Originator," Haruyuki parroted as he considered the word.

The Burst Linkers with no parents, also known as the first one hundred. Those were the Originators. They had received the Brain Burst program directly from the developer in 2039 and created the prototype of the Accelerated World.

"So then, like, does that mean all the Originators know the same stuff as Graphite Edge?" Niko asked, still lying back with her legs outstretched.

"No, I don't suppose it does." Kuroyukihime shook her head slightly. "If it was information communicated to a hundred Burst Linkers, it would have spread more. Because in the initial Accelerated World, there was no limit on the number of people who could copy and install, apparently."

"And if they made a child, naturally, they were gonna tell 'em about the conditions to clear the game. So then, I guess that means that Graphite does have some kinda secret."

"Oh, about that, Niko." Kuroyukihime cleared her throat. "I know this is me saying this, but when it comes to Graph, struggling to figure out anything he says or does is a waste of your time and processing ability. He only shows up where he wants to, he only talks about what he wants to, and he only fights the opponents he wants to. Most likely, the reason Graph chose to tell Haruyuki this information was because he's the most obedient listener in Nega Nebulus."

"O-obedient listener? What does that mean?" *Is that a compliment?* Haruyuki wondered as he asked.

"It means that you are simply obediently impressed and don't ask all sorts of questions," Kuroyukihime answered quickly.

*...That's not a compliment, is it?*

Without leaving him the chance to be disappointed, Kuroyukihime continued, "Graph intended to communicate to me through your mouth, Haruyuki, that The Fluctuating Light itself is the clear flag for Brain Burst and only that. In other words, Graph is perhaps trying to stop me from recklessly pursuing level ten."

"......!!"

Haruyuki gasped involuntarily.

Level ten. Kuroyukihime's final objective, one she would pursue even if it meant her own life as a Burst Linker. He could still viv-idly remember the words that came from her mouth in a café in Koenji the day after she gave Haruyuki Brain Burst.

*Because I put it far above friendship, above honor...becoming level ten. You could even say that alone is what I lived for.*

*I want to know. Whatever it takes, I have to know. Isn't...isn't there something beyond this? This...shell called a human being... outside...something more...*

"Kuroyukihime." Haruyuki ever so timidly asked his sword-master in a hoarse voice, "If it's like Graph says and level ten is just a checkpoint...If the final objective of Brain Burst is The Fluctuating Light in the Castle, would you stop trying for level ten?" He himself didn't really know what answer he hoped for from her.

The path toward level ten was blood-soaked and ruthless. She would have to drive four other level niners to total point loss, and it was entirely possible that *she* would end up at total point loss in the process. It hurt his heart to think about Kuroyukihime incurring so much rage and enmity, and of course, he didn't want to even think about the counterattacks against her.

But he also didn't want to watch her throw away what she had been so desperately working toward, based on the logical judg-ment that it was too dangerous or that it wasn't necessary. She cut down any and all obstacles in her path with her blades and the maddening passion within them to charge forward. Haruyuki was helplessly drawn to this powerful figure, and he was sure the other Legion members felt the same.

Conflicting feelings in his heart, Haruyuki clenched both of his hands in front of him.

Kuroyukihime blinked once at him before smoothly replying, "Impossible. Whatever the reason Brain Burst was created, I have absolutely no intention of standing still at level nine."

"Y-you don't?" Haruyuki wasn't sure whether it was okay to be relieved or not.

"The system message when I reached level nine was a challenge from the developer." Kuroyukihime favored him with a bold smile. "I am indeed interested in the reason Brain Burst was created, and I do want to know the true nature of The Fluctuating Light. And I also have the simple desire to clear this game. But above all else, I want to meet the developer and ask them directly—no, question them. What is Brain Burst? What were you thinking when you made such a thing?" Kuroyukihime opened and closed the fingers of her raised hand while Haruyuki looked on.

Abruptly, Niko chuckled. "Kuroyuki, so basically that, then? You wanna fight the developer, yeah?"

"Aah." Kuroyukihime looked like Niko had caught her with her guard down and then also laughed briefly. "Perhaps. If I could ball up and pummel the developer with everything I've experienced since I became a Burst Linker, it would certainly be a relief."

"Let me jump in when ya do. Once you're done chopping 'em up, I'll burn 'em to ash."

The two kings had innocent looks on their faces during this dangerous exchange, and then they burst into bright laughter. The corners of even Pard's mouth loosened, so Haruyuki allowed himself to be swept up in the laughter. But at the same time, he couldn't help but break into a cold sweat.

Later, the four went to pick up some things in the ground floor shopping mall before making supper together. On the menu was chilled *tantan* ramen with plenty of black sesame seeds, decided upon by Niko and Kuroyukihime because the colors were black and red. He thought this might have been a bit of a cooking challenge with this lineup, but Pard showed a surprising chef's flair, and their dinner turned out exactly like the photo on the recipe site they had referenced.

The main topic of conversation while they ate was the trip to Yamagata planned for the beginning of August, and they filled the table with holowindows, chatting excitedly about how they wanted to go here or see that, which was a lot of fun. And the black sesame chilled *tantan* ramen was shockingly delicious. The time flew by in the blink of an eye.

After Haruyuki saw Niko and Pard, who would be going home by motorcycle, and Kuroyukihime, returning home in a taxi, to the sidewalk of Kannana Street, he didn't feel like going back to his empty house right away, so he bought a drink from the vending machine and then set himself down on a bench in the shopping mall galleria on the first floor.

Eight o'clock came and went, and shoppers carrying multi-colored paper bags and residents of the condo returning home passed back and forth along the large galleria. As he stared absently at this scene, Haruyuki heard Graphite Edge's voice in his ears once again, his reply to Haruyuki's question about what would happen if The Fluctuating Light was freed.

*But if there was one thing I could say...I think the outcome will change the world.*

What did that mean—the real world would change? Would a technology that surpassed the standards for the current year of 2047 be revealed just like with the Brain Burst program itself? Or would something happen with the social camera network, given the close connection there with BB?

Haruyuki threw his head back and looked up at the black sphere placed basically in the center of the ceiling. The social camera, red indicator light blinking slowly inside the shell, was almost like the eyeball of a large Enemy.

Now that he was thinking about it, how could Brain Burst so easily hack into the social camera network, with the most critical security infrastructure in the country? Graphite Edge hadn't explained that, either. Kuroyukihime said she would type up the information from Graph, together with the matter of the Legion merger, and distribute it to the other Legion members, so Takumu might figure out a bunch of things from that. In fact, if it had been Takumu who heard Graph's story, there was no way he would've been "simply obediently impressed." These thoughts running through his mind, he continued to stare at the black camera.

"What are you doing, Haru? Sitting here like this."

He heard a voice from outside his field of view and jerked his head back down.

Standing in front of the bench was his childhood friend, shouldering a bamboo sword case—the very Takumu Mayuzumi himself, in his school uniform.

"Oh, Taku. Hey, you're home." Haruyuki hurriedly moved to stand, but Takumu checked him with a hand and then sat down to his right.

"Yeah, I'm home." He slipped the sword case off his shoulder and let out a sigh. "Aah, practice was tough today. I don't want to get back up again."

"Ha-ha! It must've been seriously hard if *you're* out of energy. Oh, here! Have this." Haruyuki handed him the bottle of rooibos tea he'd bought but still hadn't opened.

Perhaps Takumu was quite thirsty; he accepted it with a simple "Thanks," twisted the cap, and gulped about half of it down immediately. "Aah, this is giving me life...Sorry for taking it from you."

"NP. You think you'll win at the meet?"

"Ha-ha! Won't know until I get there. Well, since I'm making a showing, even if I don't win the individual fights or the group fights, I still want to go for a spot in the national meet. And..." Here, Takumu cut himself off and gripped the bottle with both hands.

"And?" Haruyuki prompted.

"Oh, uh...It's kinda embarrassing to say, but I have to win as many matches as I can in front of Nomi without relying on acceleration."

"...Right." Haruyuki relaxed his mouth and nodded.

The Twilight Marauder Dusk Taker, aka Seiji Nomi, had lost all his Burst Points in a decisive battle against Haruyuki and Takumu three months earlier, leading to the loss of the Brain

Burst program and any memory related to it. Now that he was an average seventh grader again, he adored his older teammate Takumu and worked hard on the kendo team. The Nomi of the present didn't know anything about acceleration, so Takumu's efforts were perhaps one-sided. But there was no doubt something in those efforts that would reach Nomi.

"For his sake, too, we totally have to win in the Territories on Saturday and crush the Acceleration Research Society," Haruyuki said.

"Yeah, we do." Takumu nodded deeply. "I'm actually feeling more pressure about that than the meet the next day."

"What? The next day?"

"Yes! The Territories are the day after tomorrow, and the meet's on the twenty-first. So I keep telling myself that if we can win against the White Legion, I can win at the meet, too."

"Huh," Haruyuki said. "Yeah, I guess so. I mean, the kendo meet's not all easy or whatever, but I seriously doubt there's a school team out there scarier than Oscillatory."

"Right, exactly. And the Green King the other day, too. After fighting a real high ranker in the Accelerated World, I can actually relax at something like a kendo meet. So although I'm scared that some fierce Oscillatory warrior'll show up in the Territories, I'm also excited about it," Takumu said, pushing up the bridge of his glasses.

"I get that." Haruyuki looked at his handsome face in profile with admiration. "Okay! When I'm nervous about something in the real world, I'll just try remembering when I fought a king or a super-class Enemy or something."

"So, like, when would you be nervous?" Takumu asked, and Haruyuki sank into thought.

Right before a test, he would get so nervous that his palms would sweat, but once it actually started, he would inevitably get so desperate he'd forget he was nervous. And he was a lot less nervous talking with students other than Takumu and Chiyuri in class now that they were at the end of the first term of eighth grade.

A few hours earlier, when Niko and Kuroyukihime had been

together at his house, *that* had made him pretty nervous, but if he told Takumu that, he didn't know what kind of reaction he'd get, so he decided to keep quiet. Now that he was thinking about it, though, the Haruyuki who belonged to the Animal Care Club would never actually have the opportunity to be in a sports meet of any kind in the real world, so he guessed that it was basically just when he had to speak in front of a lot of people.

Here, Haruyuki remembered he had an important proposal to discuss with Takumu and briefly cried in dismay, "Ah!"

"Wh-what's wrong, Haru?" Takumu wondered in surprise.

Haruyuki scratched his head for a second before opening his mouth. "Um. This has nothing to do with what we're talking about—well, maybe it does a little bit, but...Taku, so like, I...I think I'm gonna do it."

Even though Haruyuki had left out the object of that sentence, Takumu being Takumu had apparently understood exactly what he meant with the psychic power of a childhood friend. He opened his eyes wide for a second before grinning and nodding forcefully. "You are? Then you gotta go talk to Ikuzawa right away tomorrow."

"Y-yeah. I do...right?"

"Of course. This is gonna be fun, Haru." Still smiling, Takumu patted Haruyuki's shoulder.

Ten days earlier, Mayu Ikuzawa, the class representative for eighth grade class C, had sounded Takumu and Haruyuki out about running for election for the student council in the new term. He'd put off giving her an answer for a fairly long time, but this was the second most important decision of his life—the first, of course, being when he accepted the installation of the BB program Kuroyukihime sent him—and he'd absolutely needed this much time to firm up his resolve.

But once he told Mayu Ikuzawa yes, there would be no taking it back. Ikuzawa admired the current vice president Kuroyukihime, and she had confessed that her motivation for running in the election was because she wanted to live like her. For Ikuzawa's sake, too, Haruyuki would have to expend every effort until the election in September.

"I'm going to do everything I can to win," he declared, although his voice was just a little wobbly.

Takumu squeezed Haruyuki's shoulder and nodded. "Yeah, let's go hard, Haru. In the Territories on Saturday...and in the second-term student council election."

"And you in the meet and then at nationals!" Haruyuki added.

"Of course," Takumu replied with a smile.

After saying good-bye to Takumu in the elevator hall and returning to his own condo, Haruyuki took an hour to finish his homework and then washed up with a quick shower instead of a bath before getting into bed.

It had been a very long day. Given that he'd spent over ten hours in the Castle, it was only natural, but he'd jammed far too much information into his head during the long hours as well, and he still hadn't finished processing it all. Staring up at the ceiling in his dark room, it seemed that words like *The Fluctuating Light* and *Legion merger* and *student council election* were whirling around in the corner of his vision.

*If I fall asleep like this, I'm probably going to have weird dreams,* he thought as his exhaustion finally forced his eyelids down, and Haruyuki dropped into sleep, forgetting to even take his Neurolinker off.

And then, as predicted, he had a strange dream.

The entire sky was filled with stars. Above his head, where he stood on an invisible horizon, the countless points of light formed clusters like spherical galaxies, shining brilliantly. It wasn't as though the stars were standing still; one would move randomly, collide with another, and then *that* star would move and hit yet another star. There was something almost organic about their activity.

*     *     *

He had seen this before.

"The Main Visualizer?" he murmured. There was no one there to answer him, but Haruyuki was certain.

It had been on June 19—exactly a month ago. Although Takumu had annihilated his enemies when given an ISS kit by Magenta Scissor, he had been taken prisoner by the dark power. That night, Haruyuki had fallen asleep with a wired connection between himself, Takumu, and Chiyuri, and had visited this space, dragged along by the unconscious Takumu.

This was the central server for Brain Burst, also known as the Main Visualizer, where all calculations in the Accelerated World were performed. If the Highest Level was the place where the entire world could be seen, then this space was perhaps the place where the true nature of the Accelerated World could be glimpsed.

But it wasn't like he was equipped with an ISS kit, so why would he have wandered in here during his sleep once again? Or was this…?

"A real dream?" he muttered as he looked down at himself and patted at the hazy, transparent avatar of Silver Crow with both hands.

"This is not a dream." He heard a voice from behind and whirled around. "Although I do not know exactly what these 'dreams' you little warriors have when your mental circuits are made to rest are…I know—you will show me right here and now, servant."

There could only be one person making such absurd demands in such a haughty tone.

"M-M-M-Metatron?!" The reason Haruyuki squealed was not only because the Legend-class Enemy crowned with the name of an archangel had surprised him there. Rather than the usual small, 3-D icon shining faintly before his eyes was instead the figure of a girl so beautiful it was divine, with snowy-white wings and clad in a long dress. "Th-that form…Metatron, are your wounds healed?! So you're okay now?!"

Unconsciously, he stretched his arms out to embrace her slender shoulders. Silver Crow's hands and Metatron's body were both semitransparent, but even so, he felt a hazy warmth from her, and he was so deeply moved that he started to hug her with all his might.

Eyes still closed, Metatron swiftly raised a hand and thrust a fingertip into the middle of Haruyuki's face. "Wh-what manner of behavior is this, servant?! Do you consider this sort of insolent action to be appropriate for a servant?!"

"Hyah…I-I'm sorry…I was just so happy, I just…"

"And the recovery of my true form is not yet complete! Most likely, this space is a different phase from the Highest Level…If the phase I visited with you could be expressed as the data positioning, then this shows the data movement. Thus, I am depicted in this form, I suppose." Although she had refused Haruyuki's embrace, the Archangel didn't try to move away from him as she looked up at the oscillating galaxy.

"If you still don't have your power back," Haruyuki said, "then how did you call me to this space?"

"To use the words of you little warriors, it was 'the result of training.'"

"Tr-training?! What kind of training?" Haruyuki stared at Metatron, dumbfounded.

She opened her eyes the slightest bit and cleared her throat. "I have spent long hours enhancing the link that has been established between you and me in order to make it more certain. As a result, when all the conditions are met, I am now able to call you like this…That's all."

"W-wow…"

"Well, the enhancement is still needing much more improvement."

"W-wow…" After being obediently impressed, he started reeling. "Uh, um, that's, when you're done enhancing the link, I wonder what'll happen."

The Archangel chuckled proudly. "My ultimate objective is to be able to visit the Lowest Level where you live."

"Wh-whaaaaat?!" He threw his head back even farther, and this time, it was Metatron grabbing hold of his shoulders.

"What is that reaction exactly? Are you expressing your overabundant joy, servant?"

"O-oh, uh…I-I'd definitely be happy if you could come to my house, Metatron. Very." As he spoke, he imagined running into his mother and shuddered all over.

The look on Metatron's face grew even more suspicious, but eventually she laughed again. "It will take much more work to enhance the link before that becomes possible. I permit you to look forward to the day, Silver Crow."

"Yeah. I'm looking forward to it. Totally," Haruyuki replied obediently, before moving away from Metatron to look up at the galaxy of information once more.

When he sat down on the spot, the Archangel also lowered herself down next to him. For a while, they stared wordlessly at the flickering stars. Right around the time when he'd lost track of how long they'd been sitting there, Haruyuki asked, "Metatron? What do you think about the stuff Graphite Edge said in the Castle?"

Unusually, it took a while before her response came back to him. "I am deeply grateful that you could lead me into the Castle. However, the information input in that space is much too fragmentary, so I have not yet reached a conclusion. No…perhaps I should say that there is still insufficient data required to reach a conclusion."

"Insufficient…Yeah, I get that. And I feel like Graph didn't tell us the key parts. But…in that case, why didn't you ask Graph anything yourself?"

"Mmm." She paused again before murmuring, "I shall admit it. I was on guard against that little warrior."

"O-on guard?"

"It's not that I felt malice or ill will…He is different from the enemy who dragged me out of my palace. But something… Something—including that warrior—put me on guard. Even to simply name myself required some courage, albeit only a minute amount...It is impossible, but that warrior is...perhaps even greater than a Divine such as myself..." Metatron's voice gradually faded until she broke off entirely.

When he turned his gaze toward her, the Archangel grabbed his head with her hand and roughly pushed it down, as if to say *Don't look at me.* This inevitably set his head on her knees, but for some reason, the usual "Insolent creature!" did not come down on him, so he stayed where he was.

He could feel her soft warmth even through the helmet of his duel avatar, and a powerful desire to sleep came over him. *But I wanted to talk more about stuff,* he thought as his eyelids became so heavy he could hardly stand it.

"Someday, I will visit the Castle with you and meet him once more, I suppose. At that time, all mysteries will be revealed, and we will learn the meaning of our existence." Metatron's words echoed softly like a lullaby. "Go to sleep now, Silver Crow. And ready yourself for the fight to come..."

Listening to the stars' faint orchestra of bells from Metatron's lap, Haruyuki was consumed by a dark sleep.

# 7

Perhaps because he slept in the most irregular place in the most irregular way, even after Haruyuki's alarm woke him up, his head was full of cotton. As his mind gradually shook free of the fluffy stuffing, fragments of the strange conversation he'd had with Metatron under the starry sky came back to him, and he looked around, still lying in bed. The Archangel was nowhere in his room with the morning sunlight pouring in, and he felt half disappointed, half relieved as he got up.

He washed his face and chased away the lingering remnants of sleep with a large yawn as he opened the door to the living room where he found an unexpected guest, and his eyes widened in surprise.

No, not a guest. In fact, it was the owner of this residence and the master of the house. The woman in a blouse at the dining table flicking through the morning paper was Saya Arita—Haruyuki's mother.

"'M-morning, Mom."

Saya glanced back. "'Morning," she responded briefly before turning back to her newspaper. From her slightly exhausted appearance, she wasn't about to leave for work but had actually just returned home.

She worked at a foreign investment bank, in a department that was deeply involved with the financial market in the United States, and she often stayed at the office from eleven at night Japan time when the market over there opened until early morning. Even on days when she didn't have to, she would occasionally go drinking—whether this was for business or pleasure was unclear—so it was fair to say that she basically never returned home before the date had changed. Even so, it was rare for her to be this late.

"Guess you're working late every day, huh?" Haruyuki casually called out to her as he headed for the kitchen.

Saya stopped her hand once more and turned a penetrating gaze on him.

"I-is something wrong?" he asked.

"No…Nothing. Anyway, did you make this?"

He realized that Saya was holding a spoon in one hand. The bowl before her apparently contained the leftover chilled *tantan* ramen broth that Haruyuki had put in the fridge.

"Oh. Yeah. Last night with my friends…Um, that's just the broth, if you're going to eat it, the noodles—"

"It's fine like this. There's lots in it already," she said. "Friends? You mean, Takumu and Chiyuri?"

"Uh-uh. A friend from school and…" He struggled for a second with what to call Niko and Pard. "A couple friends who live in Nerima."

"Hmm." Saya looked surprised once more. "So you have friends other than Chiyuri who are good cooks, hmm? Boy? Girl?"

"Eeah. Um, uh…I—I leave that to your imagination," he mumbled, retreating into the kitchen. He put a slice of bread in the toaster and took a cup of yogurt and half a grapefruit before sitting down in front of his mother.

Fortunately, she didn't press him for an answer to her earlier question but kept moving her spoon from bowl to mouth and back as she read the paper. Eating his yogurt across from her, Haruyuki had the thought that it had been a long time since he'd seen her face properly in the light.

Her slightly lightened hair in a short bob and the sharp eye makeup hadn't changed from before. But he felt like her face had lost some of the sternness it used to have. Perhaps it was because of the morning light. Or a change in Haruyuki's own perceptions. He had the abrupt desire to talk with her more, but it wasn't like he had anything special to say. While he struggled with this, the black sesame *tantan* soup in front of her gradually disappeared.

When there was about a spoonful left, Haruyuki finally opened his mouth. "Um, Mom?"

"What?" Saya asked faintly, not taking her eyes off the newspaper holowindow.

He took a deep breath and put into words the decision he'd only made yesterday. "I was asked to run in the second-term student council election…And I think I'm going to do it."

"Hmm," Saya replied vaguely, only to lift her head slightly a moment later. "What? Student council elections?"

"Y-yeah."

"You were asked?" She frowned. "Ohh, right. You run in teams at Umesato. Who's the leader then?"

"Ikuzawa. She's the class C representative. It'd be Taku and me and one other person we don't know yet."

"Hmm." Saya cocked her head slightly to one side, and he couldn't tell from her expression exactly what she thought about Haruyuki's candidacy declaration.

He took another deep breath. "And…you were on the student council when you were at school, too, right, Mom? I was thinking whenever you have some time, I could get you to teach me the trick to giving speeches."

Saya laughed out loud, unusually for her. "All that happened so long ago, I've forgotten now. You just say whatever it is that you want to say. I mean, it's a speech for a junior high election."

"That's— I can't figure out what I want to say…"

"Then what are you going to be a council member for?" his mother asked, abruptly serious, and he unconsciously lowered his eyes.

*Because Mayu Ikuzawa invited me.*

*Because I want administrator privileges on the in-school net.*

*Because I want Kuroyukihime to approve of me.*

None of these was a lie exactly, but he felt like none of them was the fundamental reason for his decision, either. He searched the depths of his heart and put into words what popped up there. "I just...I wanted to do *something*. Something I haven't been able to do before."

A faint smile came across Saya's lips. She brought the last of the *tantan* soup to her mouth and then finished the water in her glass before speaking. "Then you can just say that. The most important thing in a speech is how much of it reaches the hearts of the people listening. If you simply lay out some grand manifesto, it'll go in one ear and out the other."

"How much...reaches...," Haruyuki murmured.

"Once you have a draft of your speech, show it to me." His mother closed her newspaper and stood up with her bowl and glass. "I'm going to bed. Thanks for the soup."

"G-good night."

After putting away her dishes, Saya Arita deftly tapped at her virtual desktop and sent five hundred yen for lunch money to Haruyuki's account before leaving the living room.

Friday, July 19, was cloudy as though the seasonal rain front had returned. His weather widget showed a 40 percent chance of precipitation from the afternoon, but since it still wasn't raining by the time lunch came, Haruyuki invited Takumu and the class rep Mayu Ikuzawa to the roof of the second school building with him.

On the way, they each bought *onigiri* and sandwiches and things in the cafeteria, but before they started to eat, he bowed his head neatly at Mayu. "Ikuzawa, I'm sorry my answer's so late."

"Uh-uh, it's fine. It's an important decision. So?" Mayu cocked her head to one side expectantly.

Haruyuki caught Takumu's eye for a moment before saying,

"I'll run together with you, Ikuzawa." He was going to follow that up with "I don't know how useful I'll be, though"—but before he could, Mayu was shouting excitedly.

"Really?! Aah, thanks!! We're gonna do this!!" A grin spread across her entire face, and then she quickly looked around. Fortunately, there were no other students on the roof. "I get it. The reason you brought us up here instead of the cafeteria was to avoid an information leak, huh?" Mayu nodded as if satisfied.

"Nah, it wasn't that." Takumu laughed cheerfully. "I think Haru was just embarrassed."

"H-hey!" he protested. "It's not *just* that. I figured if we were going to talk about election strategies, then it would be better if no one was around."

"Getting ahead of yourself there. Well anyway, let's eat lunch," Takumu urged, and Haruyuki and Mayu turned their backs to the rooftop fence and sat down on the parapet, some forty centimeters high.

"That reminds me, Ikuzawa," Haruyuki said, after taking a bite of his mentaiko *onigiri* and washing it down with some *genmai* tea. "Who's the fourth member of the team?"

"Actually, I haven't totally decided yet." Mayu shrugged as she brought her tomato-and-cheese sandwich to her mouth. "It's not that I don't have some ideas, but I was thinking, like, how can I put it...? Someone with a sharpness like you and Mayuzumi'd be good."

He unconsciously exchanged a look with Takumu on the other side of Mayu. Takumu didn't have too many angles to him, but there wasn't another student in the entire Umesato student body who was less sharp both externally and internally than Haruyuki. He unconsciously looked down at his body and its ample cushioning; Mayu shook her head in a huff.

"Uh-uh, I don't mean 'sharp' like dangerous or hard. I mean someone with lots of parts other people don't have."

"Still, Taku is one thing, but that doesn't fit me at all," he protested.

"That's not true." Mayu's serious face cut him off, and he looked up at the cloudy sky, which threatened rain at any second.

"The truth is, I think that everyone has something different from other people, something that's just theirs. But it's hard to express that to the outside world. When people think you're different from everyone else, or you're seeking attention, all kinds of bad things happen."

She looked and sounded as though she had actually experienced this herself, but then this momentary cloud vanished instantly, and Mayu looked at Haruyuki again as she continued.

"But, Arita, you upgraded the exhibit for the school festival on your own; you made yourself a candidate for the Animal Care Club. You're really working without trying to hide what you're good at or what you like."

"Oh. But I'm not actually good at either of those things. In fact, it's more like I had to do something, so I did it because I didn't have a choice, basically," he confessed.

"What's important is whether you actually *do* it. I think you're someone who does things properly, Arita. That's what I mean by sharp. In English, it wouldn't be *sharp*, but maybe *prominent*."

"P-prominent?" Haruyuki cocked his head to one side at the English word he couldn't remember studying.

"Like this." Mayu launched her memo app and smoothly spelled it out. "It means remarkable or foremost. As a noun, it's *prominence*. Maybe you've heard that before?"

"Oh," he said. "Like with the Sun."

"Yeah. It means a solar flare, but also standing out and excellence."

"Huh. I didn't know that." What popped up in the back of his mind was, of course, the Red Legion, led by Niko. There was no way of knowing what meaning the first Red King intended when he named it Prominence. But the Prominence inherited and kept safe by the second King, Niko, was going to merge with Nega Nebulus the following day, and an era would end.

And now, here was Mayu Ikuzawa teaching him the meaning

of the word Prominence. Coincidental though it might have been, it felt like some kind of fate to him. He shot a glance at Takumu again, and they nodded to each other slightly before turning back to Mayu.

"Um. I don't have that kind of confidence in myself yet, but I'm going to try to live up to your expectations, Ikuzawa," Haruyuki said. "Thanks for asking me to join you."

Mayu blinked in surprise once before nodding with force. "Yeah. Let's try hard, Arita!"

"Naturally, I'll give it everything I have, too," Takumu added from where he sat across from them.

She turned back toward him and shouted, "Thanks, Mayuzumi!" Mayu thrust a hand out to each of them, and Haruyuki and Takumu grabbed hold.

After that, they talked as they ate, and it was decided that they would each put forth a candidate for their fourth member in the middle of July. At the same time as Haruyuki finished his second *onigiri—ume bonito* flavor—a drop of water touched the tip of his nose.

"Ah! It's starting to rain." Mayu put a hand to her forehead and looked up at the sky, sandwich wrapper crumpled in one hand.

Haruyuki also tilted his head back and stared at the sun shining hazily on the other side of the gray clouds when a sudden thought struck him. "That reminds me, Ikuzawa. The group of four candidates, usually people give them something like a team name, right?"

"Oh, right. Yes. Although you just use it during the campaign. It's usually Blah Blah party or the Blah Blahs. Lots of names in the Team Blah Blah style. Registration starts in the second term, so I haven't thought about it at all yet…Arita, you got any ideas?"

"Not so much an idea as something that just occurred to me," Haruyuki said, standing up from the parapet/bench. "Just like, maybe we could make it the 'prominent' you just taught me, Ikuzawa. Team Prominent."

"Team Prominent…" Mayu followed him to her feet and rolled

the name around in her mouth a few times before breaking into a grin. "It sounds like we mean business. I like it! What d'you think, Mayuzumi?"

"I think it's good, too." Takumu grinned along with her, the light reflecting off his glasses.

Mayu bobbed her head up and down, setting her ponytail bouncing, and thrust her fist high up into the air, as though she were perhaps trying to push back the rain that had started to fall, and declared in a strident voice, "All right! Team Prominent starts now! Guys, let's make this happen!"

"Yeah!" Haruyuki and Takumu shouted in unison.

# 8

The long mail from Kuroyukihime was sent to all the Legion members immediately after the last homeroom of the first term had ended.

*I wonder if she wrote it during class...* The report was so detailed and easy to read that it sent a powerful chill up Haruyuki's spine. With a dual-part structure, the first half was about the proposal to merge with the Red Legion. The latter half was written on the topic of the Castle and the secrets of Brain Burst. It was all information that Haruyuki already knew, but even so, he read it in his seat as if in a trance.

And then someone was standing in front of his desk. When he looked, he saw it was Chiyuri Kurashima, already finished getting ready to go home.

"Haru." She leaned over. "You read Kuroyukihime's mail yet?"

"I'm just in the middle of it now...You?"

"Just the first half," she said. "And I was so surprised— Ah! Maybe you..."

"Wh-what?" he asked.

"Since you're not shouting 'Automagetting!' and falling out of your chair, I'm guessing you already knew." She stared at him. "About the merger."

"Th-that's, well…I mean, don't you have to go to practice?" He tried to change the subject.

"No practice today or tomorrow!" she yelled. "Now, come on! Come clean!"

Suddenly, Takumu was standing at her side. He also looked surprised—

Unsurprisingly—but given that they had the meet in two days, the kendo team would naturally have practice that day, so he didn't have the time to talk.

"Chii, make sure you ask Haru about everything for me, too." He raised a thumb as if to say he was leaving it all to her. "All right. I'll talk to you later." Takumu waved a hand and then trotted off.

Haruyuki watched him go before turning his face back to Chiyuri.

"'Kay," she said. "Let's get this story out of you then, hmm?"

"But basically everything I know's in the mail…"

"Then tell me about everything outside that 'basically'!"

With his childhood friend snapping this order at him, Haruyuki couldn't very well say no.

When they went outside, he found the rain had stopped at some point. After they walked around to the animal hutch in the rear courtyard, Haruyuki got out two bamboo brooms and pushed one at her.

"…What?" Chiyuri said, looking doubtful, and he grinned at her.

"In exchange for me telling you stuff, help me clean."

"…Well, fine. I guess."

Once they had finished cleaning up around the hutch, his Animal Care Club colleague Reina Izeki and the club super president Utai Shinomiya appeared.

"Oh!" Reina cried, noticing Chiyuri. "Um. Kurashima, right? Are you a new member—I mean, of the club?"

"No, just helping out today," Haruyuki replied for her.

"Oh yeah?" Reina looked disappointed.

"I'm sorry, Izeki," Chiyuri apologized. "I don't have practice today, so this guy made me help him."

Haruyuki started to feel like he was in the wrong somehow. *No, but it's not my fault at all.* He shook his head from side to side.

UI> EVEN IF IT'S JUST FOR TODAY, I'M SO HAPPY YOU'RE HERE, CHIYURI! HOO IS ALSO VERY HAPPY! Utai announced in the chat app.

The three looked over at the hutch, and the northern white-faced owl Hoo flapped his wings in a welcoming way—or so Haruyuki felt.

"Ha-ha-ha! Thanks, Hoo! So what should I do next?" Chiyuri asked.

Haruyuki thought for a second and then frowned. "Dig in the ground over there and gather worms for Hoo to eat."

"W—! W-w-w-w-worms?! N-no way! I'm not touching worms!!" Chiyuri inched backward.

"Oh! Look!" Haruyuki suddenly pointed at her feet. "There's one there!"

"Eeeeyaaaah!!" Chiyuri leapt up in an impressive power of legs from her many hours of sports practice. But once she confirmed there was nothing on the ground, her face turned beet red and she charged forward to yank Haruyuki's cheek. "You—! I'm going to rip this cheek off and feed it to Hoo!!"

"H-how-ow-ow-ow?! Horry, horry! Horhibe me!!"

Reina and Utai watched, dumbfounded, and then erupted into laugher, while Hoo called out loudly, "Hoo-hoooo!"

When the hutch was clean and Hoo fed—the food was, of course, not worms nor Haruyuki's cheek but the mouse meat Utai had prepared—Reina waved good-bye, and then the three Burst Linkers sat down next to one another on the bench near the hutch.

The fingers of Utai's hands flashed above her adorable kneecaps. UI> DID YOU BOTH READ THE MAIL FROM SACCHI?

"Yeah, mostly," Chiyuri said. "But like, Ui, listen to this! Haru here apparently already knew about the merger!"

UI> Is that true, Arita?

Chiyuri and Utai turned to stare at him, and Haruyuki hurriedly shook his head.

"N-no. I mean, knew, like, I only heard about it twelve hours ago! Uh. Last night, Kuroyukihime and Niko and Pard came to my house, okay..."

"Hmmmm."

UI> Hmmmm, indeed.

"N-no. I mean, came, like they weren't staying over. We made supper together and ate it, and then everyone went home."

"Hmmmmmm."

UI> Hmmmmmm, indeed.

Their eyes were getting cold on him, so he decided it would be best to just get right to the point.

"S-so that was the first time I heard anything about the merger, either. I guess it took Niko and Pard until yesterday to convince the two other members of the Triplex. And after that, it's just like in Kuroyukihime's mail. We won't know the details until tomorrow."

"I see. Mm-hmm," Chiyuri hummed deeply, her face finally resuming its normal expression. "But I wonder if Blaze Heart and Peach Parasol and them are going to get on board after they came and attacked Suginami that time in the Territories...I didn't actually fight them, but they were pretty serious, weren't they?"

UI> Yes. I don't think they will so easily forgive Sacchi for driving Red Rider to total point loss.

"So then," Chiyuri started. "Maybe Blaze and them'll leave the Legion when they find out about the merger."

Haruyuki nodded silently before asking the youngest and yet most senior Legion member there, "Shinomiya, what do *you* think about the merger?"

Without so much as appearing to think for a moment, Utai tapped away at her holokeyboard. UI> I have no particular

OBJECTION. WHEN I BECAME A BURST LINKER, IT WAS QUITE NORMAL FOR A LEGION TO MERGE WITH OR SPLIT FROM A NEARBY LEGION. THE REASON THE SITUATION IN THE ACCELERATED WORLD HASN'T SIGNIFICANTLY CHANGED RECENTLY IS BECAUSE THE SIX LEGIONS CONCLUDED THE MUTUAL NONAGGRESSION PACT. BUT

Her fingers stopped there for a moment, and then she continued, typing a little slower.

UI> IF THE LEGION NAME NEGA NEBULUS DISAPPEARS DUE TO THIS MERGER, I DO THINK THAT WOULD BE UNFORTUNATE. I'M SURE EVERYONE IN PROMINENCE FEELS THE SAME WAY.

"Mmm. I guess so." Chiyuri looked up at the sky, where the clouds were gradually thinning. "It's only been three months since I was let into Nega Nebulus, but even so, I seriously love the Legion. I do think we have to defeat the Acceleration Research Society, and I'm happy to have a whole bunch of new comrades, but...But I guess I'd be lying if I said I wasn't worried. I want to have fun with people I love in a comfortable place forever. It's just this feeling I have..."

Haruyuki unconsciously stared at the face of his childhood friend in profile. He had once told Chiyuri that the energy source for Lime Bell's special attack Citron Call was her longing for the past. The sound of the bell when she activated her technique was exactly the same as the bell at the elementary school she, Haruyuki, and Takumu had attended. Most likely, even now, she held the desire deep in the depths of her heart to return to the days when the three of them would get all sweaty running around and playing every evening, back when she wasn't afraid of a recurrence of her father's illness. Large changes like a Legion merger or a decisive battle with the Society probably made her feel more overwhelmed than he could imagine.

"It'll be okay, Chiyu," Haruyuki said. "Even if the name changes when the Legions merge, none of the important stuff'll change, y'know? We're gonna join forces with Promi, take down the Acceleration Research Society, crush their plans, and clear Brain

Burst together with Kuroyukihime. That's the goal, just like it's always been."

"Mmm." Chiyuri blinked several times and then showed him her usual grin. "Right! You and I gotta get way stronger still, Haru!"

"Y-yeah, right." Haruyuki's response was somewhat inarticulate.

Utai snickered before moving her fingers. UI> Arita, I think it's about time you got it together and decided on your level-six bonus!

"Unh! ...R-right...Graph said the same thing..."

UI> What did Graph say? Utai had already read Kuroyukihime's report, so she should have known that Haruyuki and Fuko had encountered Graphite Edge in the Castle. So Haruyuki left out the preamble and just told her what the man had said.

"Um. He said if I wasn't satisfied with how I am, I can get stronger with more training or level-up bonuses. I don't know if I'm actually unsatisfied with Silver Crow's status, though."

Chiyuri shook her head as though exasperated, while Utai smiled once again.

UI> I do recommend that you let 90 percent of what Graph says slide, but that advice is possibly part of the remaining 10 percent. If you feel a wall in the growth of your duel avatar, one idea is to change the direction of your bonuses. I'm also thinking of enhancing my close-range fighting ability next.

Haruyuki read the words Utai tapped into the chat window with great interest and sank into thought. The reason he had poured all of his level-up bonuses into enhancing his flight ability was because he had been following Kuroyukihime's advice. His resolve had been shaken when he was presented with an appealing special attack as a choice at level two, but ever since, he'd chosen to enhance his flight ability without hesitation. And yet, when it came to his level-six bonus, he felt this insurmountable reluctance...

"Graph and Master Fuko said that if it's an enemy you can't

beat alone, beat with two. And if two can't win, you just have to win with three," Haruyuki murmured, looking down at his own hands. "But I want to win alone, whatever it takes. I think there are some places where you *have* to win. And for those times, I want just a little more power. Maybe it's wrong to think like that."

UI> THAT IS THE ETERNAL STRUGGLE FOR ALL BURST LINKERS GIVEN SUPPORTIVE-TYPE DUEL AVATARS, Utai announced without a moment's delay.

Haruyuki yanked his face up. Utai was smiling, and Chiyuri was grinning. When he thought about it, Ardor Maiden was a support-type duel avatar that specialized in long-distance firepower attacks, and Lime Bell was a completely supportive type with only a simple smashing attack as her direct attack.

"Ah. S-sorry, Chiyu, Shinomiya." Haruyuki hurriedly dipped his head.

Chiyuri sputtered with laughter. "You don't have to apologize. I mean, it's like Ui said. Sometimes you wish you had more attack power. I like my avatar, and it's way more fun fighting together with everyone than it is to solo fight. I get plenty of fighting on my own in the real world at track, so I'm fine with going all out with team fights in the Accelerated World."

Utai moved her fingers nimbly. UI> YOUR WAY OF THINKING IS VERY SOLID, CHIYURI!

"When you say stuff like that, it's like I'm going in circles here," he muttered before slowly nodding. "But I totally get what you're trying to say, Chiyu. Basically, that's what I'm looking for... And I feel like Kuroyukihime also told me way back in the beginning to ask my own avatar for the answers."

UI> THAT'S EXACTLY RIGHT. I THINK IT'S BEST IF YOU CONSIDER ALL YOUR OPTIONS, STRUGGLE WITH THEM, AND THEN MOVE FORWARD THE WAY YOU TRULY DESIRE.

"Yeah, thanks, Shinomiya, Chiyu. I'll decide on my bonus before the Territories tomorrow. And...this wasn't in Kuroyukihime's report, but Graph had a message for you, Shinomiya."

Utai cocked her head to one side, and Haruyuki gave her the message entrusted to him by Graphite Edge immediately before the escape from the Castle.

"'When I escape from the Castle's north gate, I'm counting on your help, Denden'…is what he said."

Utai looked at him with wide eyes for a moment until finally she pursed her lips. UI> I DO WISH HE'D STOP CALLING ME DEN-DEN ALREADY. She typed only that before clenching her small hands into tight fists and turning her gaze upward.

When Haruyuki also looked up at the sky, a ray of golden light stretched out through a gap in the clouds to make the humid sky glitter and shine.

# 9

Of all the twenty-three wards in Tokyo, the most populous was Setagaya—or so Shihoko Nago had been repeatedly taught since elementary school in her social studies lessons. In terms of area, it was just barely second after Ota Ward, but that was because the enormous plot of reclaimed land known as Haneda Airport was in Ota. If you didn't count the airport, then Setagaya was the largest—so went the piece of trivia that had wormed its way into her brain. Thus, the thing that surprised her the most when she became a Burst Linker was the fact that Setagaya was treated as a vacant area in the Accelerated World.

"I actually still don't really get by what logic Setagaya is a vacant area," Shihoko said in a quiet voice as the Keio Line express train rocked her back and forth.

Next to her, Satomi Mito shrugged. "I guess maybe 'cause there's nowhere famous. Kids who wanna duel are gonna gravitate toward Shibuya or Shinjuku."

"It's not true that there's nowhere famous. Setagaya has all kinds of places."

"Like where?"

"Like...Carrot Tower in Sancha."

"Plus?"

"Plus...Nikotama Rise."

"And?"

"And...Todoroki Valley and Baji Koen and the Olympic Park." Shihoko earnestly listed the famous landmarks, and Satomi grinned as she nodded at each one.

"Next time, how about we ask the Crow and them how many of those they know?" she asked.

"Would! You! Quit! That?!" Shihoko groaned and hung her head, admitting defeat. It was true that Setagaya didn't have a landmark that any resident of Tokyo would know instantly, like Ikebukuro's Sunshine City or Shinjuku's government building or Shibuya's Ravine Square. Thus, people looking for a duel didn't gravitate to the ward, and as a result, the number of Burst Linkers did not increase. She understood the logic, but she still wasn't happy about it.

"Hmm, mmm. What else is there?" Shihoko muttered to herself, not knowing when to give up.

"Shiho!" Yume Yuruki, playing around on her virtual desktop across from them, suddenly lifted her face, her glasses glinting. "There is one! A famous place!"

"Huh? Where, where?"

"That massive gas tank in Roka Park."

"...That's gonna be taken down next year. And anyway, it's just a big round thing." Her shoulders slumped in disappointment, but then she straightened up again; this was no time for this sort of comedy routine. The reason they were on the Keio Line on a weekday after school when they normally walked was not to go off and have fun. It was a sortie for an important mission.

"Look," she said. "We're almost past Kanpachi now. You both cut your global connections, right?"

"Yup" came from Satomi.

"Courso" came from Yume.

Ring Road No. 8 that cut through Setagaya ward north-south was also the boundary of the area. The Shikishima University–affiliated Sakurami Junior High School they attended was in Setagaya Area No. 2. Riding the outward Keio Line train from the nearest station, Sakurajosui, they would be in Setagaya Area No. 5 once they crossed Kanpachi. Because they had turned the global-net connection on their Neurolinkers off once they got on the train, there was no chance of being challenged once the area changed. But the instant the express train racing along the elevated tracks cut across the main road, a nervousness rose up from the bottom of her stomach.

Their destination was the next station, Chitose-Karasuyama. But they weren't going shopping or anything like that. The three Burst Linkers were crossing an area boundary to challenge someone for basically the first time since they'd become Burst Linkers.

"Don't be so nervous, Shiho," Satomi said. "I mean, it's not like our opponent's definitely gonna be on the list anyway."

"In fact, it's pretty likely she won't be!" Yume chimed in.

"Yeah." She nodded slowly. "But like, I just have this feeling. Like we're gonna get to see her today."

"Right. We might. You decide what you're gonna talk about if we do?" Satomi asked.

This time, she shook her head. "Uh-uh. Not at all. But I'm sure Corvus'd say if we just go head-on with her, we'll get our message across."

"Heh-heh-heh." Yume chuckled strangely. "Yeah, maybe."

Shihoko glared at her. "I'm telling you this now. If I lose, Sato, Yume, you gotta go up against her!"

"Yeah, yeah."

"Sure, sure."

Both sounded as laid-back as ever, but only because they were trying to get the girl to relax a little. To show them her gratitude, she grabbed hold of the sleeves of their uniforms and turned her gaze out the window.

A minute later, the train gradually decelerated and slid up to the platform of Chitose-Karasuyama station. They went down the stairs out the south exit where there was a plaza in front of the station. Several benches were set out around the green space, so it looked like a good place for accelerating.

"I was thinking a café or something, but maybe the plaza's good?" Shihoko suggested, and Satomi and Yume nodded. To replenish their energy for the duel, they each got a regular cone at the ice cream shop inside the station building and then moved out to the plaza. Once they sat down alongside one another on a bench farther in under the shade of a tree, the three wordlessly enjoyed their snacks for a while.

When Shihoko's strawberry cheesecake, Satomi's cookies and cream, and Yume's *dainagon azuki* bean ice cream disappeared at the same time, they all nodded at one another and reached a hand toward their Neurolinkers to push the button for a global connection.

Since they'd already had a meeting in advance and determined that Shihoko would duel first, while Satomi and Yume stayed in the Gallery, it was only Shihoko who accelerated. She took a deep breath. "Burst Link!!"

*Skreeeee!* The sound echoed in her mind, and the summer evening froze a pale blue. She moved into the initial acceleration space of the Blue World in her full-dive avatar, modeled after Gretel from Grimms' fairy tales, and tapped the B icon burning a bright red on her virtual desktop. Feeling equal parts excitement and dread, she opened the matching list.

Par for the course in an area that was known as vacant, there were only two names on the list other than Plum Flipper and Mint Mitten. The instant she identified the string of letters on top of the list, her breath stopped, even though she was in the middle of a full dive.

MAGENTA SCISSOR. The terrifying radical who had forcefully infected some dozen Burst Linkers, including Satomi and Yume, with ISS kits as part of a plan to level the playing field in the Accelerated World. The very person Shihoko had come to see. She'd been told her headquarters were Setagaya Area No. 5, but she supposed it was a stroke of good fortune that she had suddenly come across her like this.

But the matching list also contained some unexpected information. The other avatar name displayed right below Magenta's.

Avocado Avoider. The supersized avatar who had paired up with Magenta. And the names of Magenta and Avocado were connected by a mark indicating that they were a tag team.

"Tag!" Shihoko murmured, her index finger hovering above the list. A tag team couldn't challenge a solo Burst Linker, but the opposite was allowed, so Shihoko taking on Magenta and Avocado was possible in terms of the rules. But if they ended up fighting, her chances of winning would drop dramatically.

"What should I do…?" Biting her lip, she glanced to one side, but of course, she got no answer from the frozen, blue Satomi and Yume.

She could stop her acceleration for the moment and register as a tag team with one of them before once again challenging Magenta. But during that minute or so, Magenta might disappear from the list, and then it would all be for nothing.

Shihoko made her fairy-tale avatar look back and up at the northern sky. About a kilometer north of the Keio Line's overhead tracks, the Chuo Expressway ran east-west. Beyond that was Suginami, the territory of Nega Nebulus, which Shihoko and her friends had joined three days earlier.

*What would Silver Crow do at a time like this?* Shihoko thought, only to abruptly giggle.

After school three days earlier, in the student council office of the private Umesato Junior High School near Shin-Koenji station, Shihoko and her two friends had come face-to-face with the members of Nega Nebulus in the real for the first time. Unfortunately, not all of Nega Nebulus was in attendance—it had only been five of them: the Legion Master, Black Lotus (aka Kuroyukihime), Ardor Maiden (one Utai Shinomiya), Cyan Pile (Takumu Mayuzumi), Lime Bell (Chiyuri Kurashima), and Silver Crow (Haruyuki Arita). But apparently, Shihoko and her friends would be introduced to the remaining Sky Raker and Aqua Current soon.

MAGENTA SCISSOR

The one who made the deepest impression was, of course, Master Kuroyukihime. Shihoko couldn't help but be overwhelmed by the otherworldly beauty of the Umesato student council vice president, using her handle name (?) of Kuroyukihime even in the real world, and her seemingly indefatigable (?) mental strength. Shihoko and her friends had nodded in agreement on the way home: Of course, the Black King was no ordinary person.

And then after Kuroyukihime, the second strongest impression had been made on her by Silver Crow—Haruyuki Arita. His face and body were both round, and his image was in stark contrast to his Accelerated World duel avatar. But just like when they'd met in the Unlimited Neutral Field, Shihoko's nervousness melted away in the blink of an eye. It quickly became clear to her soon that Kuroyukihime and the others trusted him a great deal.

If it was Silver Crow...If it was him, with the strength to always accept his own weaknesses and push forward with all his might, he probably wouldn't blanch at his opponent turning out to be a tag team.

Right...The reason Shihoko was in Setagaya wasn't simply to fight and win. She had come this far to share something more important than victory with her former enemy.

"Satomi, Yume. And Corvus. I...I'm gonna do it!" Shihoko shouted in the frozen-blue world and punched the matching list button.

As she transformed from her Gretel avatar into her duel avatar, Chocolat Puppeter, Shihoko fell through the darkness until she landed on solid ground—no, until her feet were swallowed up by a shallow layer of water. Aware of waves lapping ticklishly at her ankles, she slowly opened her eyes. Instantly, the powerful sunlight dyed her field of view white.

She quickly adjusted the sensitivity of her eye lenses, and color returned to the world. Blue water stretched out endlessly. It was only about ten centimeters deep, but it covered the entire field.

All the buildings had been turned into skeletal concrete frames bleached white in the sun, and the wind that blew between them swept up little wavelets on the water surface.

The natural-type, water-attribute Water stage. It was quite popular thanks to the bright sun and clear water, a design that allowed players to taste a bit of the resort life. But the instant Shihoko recognized the stage, she muttered, "Oh, crud." But regardless, the duel had started. And by Shihoko challenging. All she could do now was fight with everything she had.

First, she checked on the situation. There were two health gauges displayed in the top right of her field of view, one upon the other. As expected, the one on top was Magenta Scissor, while the one below was Avocado Avoider.

There were also two guide cursors in the lower center of her vision. But they were indicating different directions. It seemed that Magenta and Avocado were in different places within the area. The one she was supposed to meet was Magenta, but she didn't know which cursor was pointing toward her.

Finally, she spun around to take a look at her surroundings and saw the figures of the two members of the Gallery on the roof of the station building a little ways off. Of course, it was Mint and Plum. As Shihoko raised a hand to wave, they both jumped down.

After landing gently without sending any water spraying up, Satomi and Yume ran directly over to her, shouting alternately.

"What'll we do, Choco?!"

"You're up against a tag team?!"

"Why didn't you just reaccelerate?!"

"And they're level six and five, you know?!"

As the two interrogated her, she glanced at her own health gauge. The level displayed beside her avatar name was five, the same as Avocado. The power gap from the opposing tag team was absolute. But.

"Min-Min, Pliko. Listen?! A Burst Linker! Once she accelerates, all that's left is to fight in earnest! She must!!"

"《《《　　》》》"
......

Satomi and Yume fell silent, dubious looks on their faces.

"If you would think that *I* would shrink in the face of a tag team of a mere five and six, then you are greatly mistaken!" she declared in an even higher-pitched voice. "I will neatly defeat them both and happily accept the many points I earn!"

"But, Choco, you didn't come to duel—," Satomi started, but she didn't get to finish.

Suddenly, her friends vanished from before her eyes. They'd been forcibly moved due to the fact that a dueler other than a parent or Legion member had approached to within a ten-meter circle. Shihoko quickly looked back.

*Splsh!* Meager waves rippled outward from the center of the station plaza where a human figure had descended to stand. Slender and tall. The F-type avatar silhouette was wrapped in reddish-purple, ribbon-type armor. Weapons like large knives were equipped on each hip, and the only body part exposed was the mouth, where a bewitching smile played.

The duel avatar was without a doubt Magenta Scissor. But there was just one thing that was different from the last time Shihoko had encountered her. She had no jet-black eyeball-type Enhanced Armament attached to the center of her chest—no ISS kit.

Her red lips moved, and Shihoko heard a husky voice. "I was wondering who'd come to challenge us in an area like this. If it isn't our neighbor, Choco."

Pushing back her nerves, Shihoko returned resolutely, "Unfortunately, my headquarters is no longer Setagaya Number Four."

"Oh my! Did you move?"

"I did not!" She took a deep breath, threw out her chest, and named herself. "I am now Chocolat Puppeter of the Legion Nega Nebulus!"

The smile on Magenta's lips faded somewhat. "Hmm. So you came all this way to tell me of your Legion transfer?"

"To be precise, it was not a Legion transfer. Petit Paquet was disbanded, and Min-Min, Pliko, and I all joined Nega Nebulus!"

Shihoko announced, and Magenta's faint smile disappeared altogether. She didn't know if this was because the other Burst Linker was mad or exasperated or annoyed at the way Shihoko spoke.

Her somewhat formal tone was not because she was trying to create a particular character or use psychological warfare. At some point, she had become unable to speak any other way, no matter how she tried, when she was Chocolat Puppeter. Or rather, it was perhaps more accurate to say that once this tone had sunk into her, she'd finally been able to act naturally and fight in the Accelerated World. Satomi and Yume would sometimes tease her, but Shihoko surprisingly didn't hate this self of hers. At the very least, she was far more free to speak her mind without fear than she was in the real world.

Right. She was here to speak. The reason she'd come to that area that day, the reason she'd challenged Magenta Scissor. Shihoko steeled her will and started to open her mouth.

But an instant before she could, Magenta said in an even cooler voice, "So then, you came to warn me? To say that the three of you are members of the Black Legion now, so I won't get off so easily if I lay a hand on you?"

"Pardon?" Surprised into speechlessness, she clenched her hands into fists and indicated her denial of this with her whole body. "Wh-why, that's not it at all!"

"So then, is this a pilgrimage or what? Did you come to get revenge on me for the ISS kit thing?"

"Th-that is even more incorrect! You have the whole situation wrong!" Shihoko shook her head so forcefully that her bonnet threatened to go flying. "It is true that I won't so easily forget the fact that you forcefully parasitized Min-Min and Pliko with the ISS kits, or that you tried to hunt our friend Coolu. However…Silver Crow told me how you helped him and the others in the end, in the battle to destroy the ISS kit main body."

Magenta's lips curled with dissatisfaction. "That story's gotten a bit exaggerated, it seems. I wasn't helping Crow; I was just trying to protect my comrades."

"That's fine, too. If you have the desire to protect your comrades… then that means you're a Burst Linker just like us." Shihoko had gotten that far when the water at Magenta Scissor's feet scattered in an explosion of white spray.

With a fierce charge, Magenta closed the distance between them at once. Her hand flattened like a sharp sword cut through the whiteout of the spray and closed in on Shihoko's neck.

Clenching her teeth, Shihoko sank down and twisted her upper body. Magenta's strike grazed her neck with a *tch* and slipped past. Her health gauge dropped ever so slightly, and she wanted more than anything to leap back, but fleeing carelessly was deeply inadvisable at this stage.

She grabbed hold of Magenta's left arm with both hands and braced her feet firmly in the water as she threw her backward with what was essentially a one-armed shoulder throw. The taller duel avatar should have slammed into the water on her back, but she deftly did a somersault in the air and stuck the landing quite magnificently.

Here, Shihoko finally stepped back and snapped a finger at Magenta. "That is very dangerous all of the sudden…indeed!"

Magenta looked back and fortunately did not pursue the attack, but now a very clear animosity bled into her voice. "It's a duel; it's *supposed* to be dangerous. Anyway, nice job standing there and evading that. I'm a little surprised."

"I have a long history as a recluse in the Unlimited Neutral Field. I may not have very much duel experience, but I have memorized all the attack strategies in the various stages."

As she spoke, she checked the water beneath her feet. The liquid covering the Water stage was only ten centimeters deep, but in close combat, this meager water depth was more treacherous than it seemed. Players would forget that only their feet were sunk into the water, and when they carelessly tried to jump or run, they were more likely than not to fall. When moving, you first had to lower your center of gravity and make very sure of your foothold. This was the trick Shihoko had learned through painful experience from playing tag and stepping on shadows with Satomi, Yume, and Coolu.

Meanwhile, being level six, Magenta Scissor of course was familiar with this somewhat rare stage. Even without the ISS kit, Shihoko was forced to admit that she was a worthy warrior with the sharpness of her striking hand and earlier somersault. Which was exactly why she could not lose here, of all places.

"Magenta. Given that I was the one who challenged you, I have no intention of evading the fight. However…after that, I would ask that you hear what I have to say."

A thin smile rose up on Magenta's lips once more. "Well then, you'll have to try hard to keep me from taking you down. Because once this duel is over, I'm going to cut my global connection immediately."

"All right." Shihoko nodded, adding in a resolute voice, "I would ask that you also do not leave the battlefield so simply… please!"

At the same time as she finished speaking, she kicked off the ground beneath the water as hard as she could. The tips of her toes sliding along the surface, she closed the distance between them in a heartbeat.

Chocolat Puppeter's armor basically only looked like chocolate; it didn't melt in the sun or break upon impact. But even so, it was equipped with several properties based on chocolate. The most peculiar of these was the sweetness when you licked it, and her heat resistance was on the low side, but it would also repel water. Thanks to this water-repellent property, she could diminish water resistance to a certain degree in a Water stage. Dashing to close in on Magenta, Shihoko sliced through the water with a left mid-kick.

In a reaction befitting her, Magenta bent her right arm. The armor of Shihoko's leg beat down from above this guard.

*Clang!* Magenta was knocked slightly off-balance.

"Hah!" Even as she staggered, she launched a left hook in a counterattack with a sharp cry.

Shihoko sank down to dodge it and drew in close to Magenta, pressing on her opponent's neck with both hands as she stabbed her left knee into the ribboned avatar. One blow, two, and then three!

Magenta's ribbon armor perhaps didn't have such a high resistance to strikes; with the three *Ti Khao* knee strikes in succession, her health gauge dropped over 10 percent.

"Ngh." Undaunted, Magenta threw out punches with her right and left arms, but given her long reach, her movements were awkward in these close quarters. And the strikes from above were obstructed by Shihoko's large hat, so they didn't manage to reach her face.

To escape from a clinch, the standard practice was to either remove your opponent's grip from the inside with both hands or spin around to the side. But Magenta had apparently not studied that far. Still clinging to her, Shihoko took what she could of the other girl's gauge with strikes and took the lead in the fight.

As Magenta crumpled, Shihoko was just about to drive home her fourth knee kick. But then an icy shiver caressed her stomach.

Reflexively, she released her hold and shoved on her opponent's shoulder to create some distance. A silver flash raced upward in the gap that was created between them.

An icy chill shot through her, from her stomach up into her chest, and the bright-red damage effect chased after it. As she looked to see her own health gauge drop 5 percent in the corner of her eye, Shihoko jumped even farther back.

In her outstretched hand, Magenta Scissor was gripping a large knife. The tip of the blade, whipped out sharply from her right hip, had sliced effortlessly through Shihoko's armor.

Regretting how she had become utterly focused on a weaponless battle, just like when she was sparring with Satomi, Shihoko dropped into position without a word.

But Magenta slowly lowered the knife of her right hand and called out with a smile, "I'm a tad surprised. I thought you were a long-range type, and here you are surprisingly accustomed to hand-to-hand combat, hmm? Where've you been training?"

"Min-Min—Mint Mitten—goes to a martial arts dojo on the other side. She is 1.3 times stronger than I am."

Instantly, a voice came down from up on a nearby building—"Your numbers are ridiculous!"—but she decided to ignore it.

Magenta also didn't react, but instead she nodded lightly, her eyes still on Shihoko. "I see. So they're techniques you spent time learning in the real…I must apologize for not taking you seriously, then." She also removed the knife on her left hip with her other hand and spun the two weapons at top speed before snapping into a fighting position.

At first glance, it looked like she fought with a blade in each hand, but that was actually not the case. The two knives were together a single Enhanced Armament, and by fusing them, Magenta created the scissors that were the origin of her avatar name. And then she would show what she was really made of…

But Magenta didn't move to cross the two knives. "I'm gonna use this, so you can go ahead and summon them, Choco. Your delicious-looking puppets."

"I'm sorry to tell you, but my special-attack gauge is still insufficiently charged," she replied, but the truth was, her gauge was just barely full enough for her to call up one Chocopet. But sadly, she couldn't summon it right away.

That was the reason Shihoko had muttered "Oh, crud" the instant she realized it was a Water stage—she couldn't use the Cocoa Fountain special attack here, the prerequisite for summoning her Chocopets. In other words, she needed to move to a dry place to call her Chocopets, but the majority of this stage was covered with water. And the buildings were only concrete skeletons; there was no space there where she could create her Cocoa Pond.

Perhaps realizing the situation Shihoko was in or perhaps not, Magenta kept her faint smile as she spoke. "Well then, I'll charge it up a bit for you." She took a step forward, the knives in both hands glittering ominously.

Then.

The water in the plaza in front of the station rocked and surged with a wave that was not generated by the wind. Regularly, once a second, the water surface shuddered. If she listened carefully, she could also hear the showy *splash, splash* of the water.

"Oh my," Magenta murmured, retreating as she lowered her knives.

Very carefully readying herself, Shihoko also glanced in the direction of the sound.

On the road—no, the waterway—connecting with the station plaza, a silhouette was slowly approaching from the south. Despite the fact that it was still quite far away, the water shuddered and rippled due to the immense size of the shadow. A Burst Linker without forehand knowledge might have mistaken it for an Enemy, although they were not supposed to exist in the normal duel field.

Two and a half meters tall. A meter and a half wide. The massive bulk wrapped in dark-green armor was perfectly egg-shaped. Running along on short, fat legs, sending magnificent sprays of water up into the air, was none other than Magenta's partner, Avocado Avoider.

...*So we're finally getting serious here?* she murmured to herself, slowly inching backward. She had almost been literally eaten by this very Avocado once before.

A few seconds later, Avocado raced into the plaza and stood next to Magenta. No sooner had he done so than his low voice rumbled out and intensified the water's rippling. "Sorry, Magenta! I'm late!"

"It's no big deal, Avo. You're in the south of the area and all... And at any rate, I was planning to do this fight alone." She hooked her fingertip through the ring-shaped knife grip—more precisely, the handle of the scissors—and spun it around.

"No!" Avocado shook his head, together with his large body. "I...I wanna fight with you!"

"Oh yeah? But our opponent's level five, you know? And a

level five and six duo attack, well, that'd be picking on someone weaker than us."

*There is no need for concern!* Shihoko nearly shouted. But when she had gotten the "there" in her mouth, Avocado's loud voice drowned her out.

"Then I'll fight Choco by myself!" he declared, the small eye lenses on the upper part of his egg-shaped body flashing as he took a heavy step forward.

Magenta shrugged as if to say "Well, there you have it" and called out to Shihoko. "Choco, hon, sorry, but maybe you could take Avo on instead. Looks like he's really been looking forward to a rematch with you."

"I—I have no objection," she replied, but in her heart, she couldn't help thinking *Whoa, indeed.*

The truth was Chocolat Puppeter wasn't so incompatible with Magenta Scissor, although only under the condition that she was able to summon her Chocopets. Because the Chocopets, chocolate in human form, were basically immune to Magenta's blade attacks.

But it was no exaggeration to say that her compatibility with Avocado Avoider was the worst. On top of Avocado's soft armor rendering nearly all physical attacks ineffective, his large mouth was big enough to swallow her Chocopets whole, and they were weak to biting attacks. The only way she could come up with to fight him was to blow away the soft armor with an annoying string of striking attacks and yank out the true avatar body inside. And anyway, there wasn't any ground anywhere nearby for her to summon her Chocopets.

But if she lost here, she wouldn't be able to achieve her main objective of talking with Magenta.

In terms of level, and in terms of compatibility with both stage and opponent, this was indeed a fierce situation. But she had to turn those disadvantages around and fight bravely—even if she couldn't win, she had to show enough resolve to persuade

Magenta at the very least. As a member of Nega Nebulus. As one Burst Linker who loved the Accelerated World.

"All right. Come, Avocado Avoider!!" Shihoko shouted, adopting an upright posture in the style of *Muay Thai*.

Avocado raised his short arms and shouted back, "I...tried to eat you last time! But today...I win!!"

Letting out a roar, he charged in a straight line, and each time the super-heavyweight avatar stepped on the ground, columns of water shot up like a fountain.

In the back of Shihoko's mind, a fragment of a thought made a noise as it was given a singular shape. The battle with Silver Crow ten days earlier...He had grasped the terrain of the stage three dimensionally and defeated Shihoko with unexpected methods. Of course, Chocolat Puppeter didn't have the ability to fly. But she should still be able to do the same thing. To do so, first of all, she had to get the upper hand on Avocado health gauge–wise.

Shihoko stood waiting in place for the massive egg-shaped bulk charging ferociously toward her.

"Hyoooaaanh!" Avocado spread his arms and jumped. Crushing the enemy with his heavyweight body protected by thick armor was his standard move. It was simple, but the attack was hard to counter. But if she started running away in the early stages of the fight, she would lose precious time.

"Ooyah!" With a single battle cry, she took decisive action, sliding directly beneath him. Slipping along the water surface, she just barely managed to pass under the falling bulk and slip out behind him.

*Splooooosh!* The sound of water filled the air, and a fountain of spray shot up. Showered in water droplets, she turned around and flew at Avocado, who was trying to get to his feet.

It was the perfect chance for a counterattack, but any reckless kicks or punches would be absorbed by his soft armor and do no damage. Given how short his arms and legs were, they seemed sturdy; joint techniques were also hopeless.

She took careful aim and launched a blow with all her might behind it for a direct hit on the real body of the avatar inside the armor. Avocado's real body—she'd seen it once before—was a mere fifty centimeters around. This was buried in the center of the green shell that was a meter and a half around. In other words, to do damage to the real body, she had to pierce fifty centimeters of armor.

The gym that Shihoko's master Satomi went to was a so-called mixed-martial arts type, but for strikes, the foundation was *Muay Thai* techniques. Naturally, Shihoko had also been taught these, but for some reason, she'd only been given permission to use the left mid-kick, the left jump, and the right straight in a real fight. However, she had a modest pride in these techniques, given that she had practiced essentially an infinite number of times in the time that was essentially infinite in the Unlimited Neutral Field. In the Silver Crow fight before, as well, if it had been just close combat on the ground, there was also a moment when she could see that she would have taken the lead.

The trick of the right straight punch according to Satomi: Brace your left foot like *unh*, twist your right heel like *whup*, *fwwm* your right hip around, *bwam* the force of rotation and your body weight behind it—and then *kablam!* Out in a straight line like you're firing a massive gun from your right shoulder!!

Faithfully following the excessively onomatopoeiaed instructions, Shihoko launched her right straight and dug deep, ever deeper into Avocado's back as he was getting to his feet.

The soft armor, with the viscosity and elasticity of bread dough allowed to rise once, caught her fist and tried to push it back. But Chocolat Puppeter's armor was very smooth—almost Teflon—and her small fist gouged into the soft body, piercing it, and reached the avatar's naked body.

The feedback was more like she had pushed rather than punched, but Avocado's pit—or rather main body—had basically zero defensive abilities, and his health gauge dropped over 10 percent. Once she pulled her arm out, the wound was filled in, so she gave up on a follow-up attack and got some distance.

"Now I have turned the tables, Avocado!" she shouted, a sad attempt at a challenge, and made both of them check his gauge before whirling on her heel. She ran for the station building adjacent to the plaza.

"I...don't lose!" Avocado shouted from behind as he stood and set off after her in hot pursuit.

The building was only a frame, but the stairs were there just like she remembered. She flew up the bare concrete steps, racing toward the top floor. Avocado gave chase, making the entire structure shake.

The roof was a flat surface, a latticework of gaps. Satomi and Yume were at the very far edge. She stopped to respond to their cheers by striking a tough pose and then dashed in the direction of the plaza along the lattice structure.

"You won't get away, Choco!!" Avocado rushed out headlong from the staircase, roaring. He slipped a couple times, but given that he was bigger than the gaps in the latticework, he didn't fall down but rather half tripped his way over to Shihoko.

The station building was about fifteen meters tall. Although there was water below, it was shallow, so if Chocolat Puppeter fell, she wouldn't walk away unscathed. Meanwhile, Avocado would no doubt be unharmed in a fall thanks to his thick, soft armor. Which was exactly why he had chased after her without a second thought.

"Come, Avocado Avoider!!" On the northern edge of the roof, she stood on the thirty-centimeter frame and waggled the outstretched fingers of her hand beckoningly.

"I...win!!" With this simple declaration, Avocado threw his arms out and dashed toward her. His strategy was probably to grab hold of her and then fall together. This time, there was no space for her to slip underneath him, and he was nearly three meters wide with his arms out, so it would be hard to dodge to either side in front of him.

But Shihoko was calm as she stood waiting for Avocado. The massive egg filled her field of view. She could hear Satomi and Yume yelling for her to get out of the way.

Not yet. She would draw him in further. Shihoko waited until Avocado was close enough that he could no longer stop himself.

"Now!" The moment she had carefully set her sights on was here; she jumped back.

Naturally, there was no foothold there. Shihoko began to drop soundlessly. If she kept going and hit the ground, she wouldn't be able to avoid serious damage. But her hands caught onto the edge of the frame passing before her eyes, and using the force of the reaction, she swung her feet in ahead of her and yanked herself up through a gap in the lattice with something along the lines of a gymnastics move.

Directly ahead of her feet was Avocado's back. She used her toes to push him with everything she had, and the heavyweight avatar leapt from the roof.

"I'm falling!" he announced faithfully before disappearing from her sight.

Having climbed up onto the frame once again, Shihoko stared down at the falling Avocado. A second later, the massive body slammed into the water in the plaza, atomizing the liquid into jets of frothy spray. His soft armor was completely flattened, and just as she'd expected, this absorbed the majority of the impact so that Avocado was essentially unharmed.

However, this situation—this moment—was precisely what Shihoko had been aiming for. Avocado's impact had displaced enough water to lay bare a circle of tiled earth more than ten meters across. It would of course be covered again soon enough, but she only needed a few seconds.

Brandishing her hand high above her head, she turned her index finger toward the dry land and shouted, "Cocoa Fountain!!"

A shining brown pond welled up immediately next to Avocado. She yanked her finger up and yelled, "From there…Puppet Maker!!"

The pond instantly contracted, and a human shape made of

chocolate sprang forth from its center. Shihoko gave orders to the automatic doll, whose face shone with a flower pattern. "Chocopet! Evade attack!!"

Avocado had finally gotten back up. He had no sooner noticed the Chocopet standing in a defensive posture next to him than he was thrusting both hands out and opening his massive mouth. "I...eat choco!"

Since the Chocopet could only use striking techniques, it had no way of doing damage to Avocado. Meanwhile, Avocado Avoider could bite down on the avatar whole with his mouth, which was rumored to be filled with a void.

Thus, Shihoko had ordered the Chocopet to focus on evasion, but it wouldn't be able to keep that up for long. If it could keep Avocado's attention for twenty—no, ten seconds, though, that would be plenty.

From the root fifteen meters up, she stared at Avocado chasing the Chocopet. It might have been the Accelerated World, but she was honestly afraid. She'd never once jumped of her own will from somewhere this high up. But she *had* been knocked down from a place many times higher up than this. And Shihoko had learned then that while there was the risk of instant death, the vast energy that a fall from up high generated could also be a powerful weapon. Next time, she would ask Silver Crow to take her as high up as he could ascend.

She stretched out her right foot, toes pointed sharply. Below, she saw that Avocado had finally succeeded in capturing the Chocopet and was opening his large mouth to devour it.

From the edge of the plaza, Magenta Scissor, who had been watching quietly up to that point, shouted sharply, "Avo! Above!!" They were a tag team, so it wasn't particularly a breach of etiquette to give him advice. But it was too late.

*"Hanga...?"* Avocado Avoider made a strange sound as he started to look up at the sky.

And then Shihoko's foot stabbed into the top of the egg-shaped avatar. Chocolat Puppeter's slender and relatively smooth, slippery leg gouged ever deeper into Avocado's soft armor, which had defended against even the full weight of Silver Crow's spiral kick, and the tips of her toes touched the real body hidden deep inside. This time, she felt a definite sense of impact, and Avocado's health gauge dropped 20 percent all at once.

"O-ow!!" Avocado shrieked and released the Chocopet to try to grab ahold of Shihoko piercing his head. But his arms were too short and couldn't reach her. Meanwhile, Shihoko fought the peristalsis of the soft armor trying to push her leg back out and ground the tips of her toes into the main body.

"Now admit that you're in quite the bind! Otherwise, I'll make it hurt even more!" Shihoko thought about it, and then thought some more, and decided *I kind of don't like how that sounds.*

"N-no!" Avocado was flailing out of control, but he had a surprising stubborn streak. "I...will fight Choco more. More!"

"Then I guess I have no choice!" Hardening her heart, Shihoko put every bit of strength she had into a kick to smash Avocado's body.

"Avo! That's enough!!" The cry echoed across the plaza. The owner of the voice was Magenta Scissor. She was walking toward them with her arms crossed, both her knives back on her hips. Avocado froze, and Shihoko hung her head, still stabbing into the top of the other avatar.

"I lose...," Avocado announced, slumping to sit on the spot, so Shihoko pulled her foot out and jumped down from his head.

They still had half the duel time left. She stepped back together with the precious Chocopet she'd finally been able to summon and stared at the approaching Magenta. She'd managed somehow to get a victory by decision over Avocado, but Magenta was still essentially unharmed. This was the real start of the duel—or so she thought.

Magenta came to a stop next to Avocado and patted him near the top where the hole was still open as she spoke in a curt but warm voice, "You did your best there, Avo. Choco was a cut above today, but you'll be able to fight much better next time."

"Next time…," Avocado murmured, whirling around on the fulcrum of his butt. "Choco. Will you come again?"

"Uh…Um." She was unconsciously stuck for an answer, but with those tiny eye lenses staring hard at her, she got the feeling that she couldn't just simply refuse. She cleared her throat and put her hands on her hips. "W-well, if the spirit moves me, I suppose I could do you the favor of coming again."

"Yay!" Avocado Avoider waved both arms wildly. "Next time, I eat—no, win!!"

A transparent smile rose up on Magenta Scissor's face for the merest instant, a smile that quickly became challenging as she turned to look at Shihoko. "Now…what'll you do, Choco? You wanna keep the duel going with me as your opponent? Or do you want to have your chat or whatever?"

As a Burst Linker, she should perhaps reply, "I will fight, of course!" But her opponent still had plenty of energy to spare. If Magenta was willing to listen to what she had to say, then she had to take advantage of this opportunity.

"Well then, I would ask that you hear what I have to say," Shihoko responded, and Magenta waved her hand, urging her to speak then. She took a step forward and a deep breath, but then her throat closed up like it was glued shut. She frantically tried to open her mouth, but her throat was spasming so hard that she couldn't make a sound no matter how she tried.

There was no way for involuntary movement to happen to an avatar in a virtual world. It wasn't her flesh-and-blood body shrinking; it was her spirit. Right. Chocolat Puppeter's high-handed way of speaking was no doubt a mask to hide her own shyness.

Shihoko was extremely bad at handling conflict. She held her breath at school so that she wouldn't stand out, and if she sensed trouble brewing, she left the scene immediately. She feigned an agreeable smile in front of everyone, and even if something made her mad, she would never let it show. Even with her own parents, she had gotten into the habit of being one step ahead so that they wouldn't get angry with her. She thought that she let her true self out with Satomi and Yume, but that could have just been her deluding herself.

She had told her friends that the mental trauma that was the resource for her duel avatar Chocolat Puppeter was the fact that she had been allergic to chocolate since she was small, and she herself 90 percent believed that. But...what if...perhaps the armor with the scent, texture, and taste of chocolate was an expression of her desire not to be hated? Perhaps the mask of the friendly smile that Shihoko wore in the real world had produced her sweets avatar in the Accelerated World.

If that was the case, it was deeply ironic that she was finally able to act freely by wearing a high-handed and antagonistic mask with this avatar. Or was she actually just doing the same kind of performance as in the real world? Had she been stifling herself all this time in this world, too? What on earth was the "real" her?

"Magenta." Before she knew it, the stiffness had vanished from her mouth, and Shihoko spoke her former nemesis's name. "Indeed, I— The truth is: I didn't really like duels too much."

Magenta was staring hard at her. Taking in the powerful gaze emitted by the invisible eye lenses, Shihoko continued, without noticing that at some point she had adopted her usual real-world tone, "All this time, I thought it was enough if I could just have fun hanging out with my friends in this world cut off from reality. But...Brain Burst is a fighting game, so I can't keep running away from the fights forever. There's going to come a time when I'll have to fight to stay in this world. And lately, I've been thinking that you're the one who made me realize that, Magenta."

"How incredibly spoiled you are," Magenta said coolly, lips twisting up. "I mean, all of you, you fought any number of duels to reach level five, right? In the process, you stole plenty of points from other Burst Linkers. I'm not saying that's bad or anything. But now you stand here, telling me you just forgot about all the Burst Linkers you stepped on so you could pal around having fun; I mean, you gotta be kidding me."

The anger in Magenta Scissor's words cut through Shihoko's heart and made it ache painfully. But it was only natural that when one person and another person slammed their individual truths up against each other, there would be anger—and pain. They couldn't communicate their true feelings if she kept avoiding that.

"I...guess...up to now, I've only been thinking of us. I've just been like, it's fine as long as we're having fun. But after meeting you and your friends, Magenta Scissor, and Crow and them, I understand. I was given power in order to fight, and if the time comes when I should fight, then I have to fight. In order to be a Burst Linker...and to protect the things I want to protect. That feeling...it's the same for you, isn't it?"

Magenta pursed her lips tightly and raised a hand with its tapered nails, as if to grab the center of her chest covered in the ribbon armor. The place where a jet-black eye had once parasitized her. "I don't have a single thing I wanna protect in this twisted world. But if we're talking things I want to destroy, I can't even count how many of those I have," she spat, her voice like ice.

"Liar!" Shihoko shouted, putting her own hand to her chest in the same way. "At the very least, you want to protect Avocado! That's why you sought power, isn't it?!"

"Don't talk like you know me! You and your cute avatar and your powerful abilities, what would *you* know?!"

"I *do* know! I love Min-Min and Pliko, too! And that feeling has to be there inside you, too!!"

"If you say any more stupid stuff—!" Magenta's hand flashed out to clasp onto the grip of her knife.

But in that instant, Avocado Avoider opened his massive mouth and roared at an incredible volume, "I...love Magenta!!" Surprisingly large tears spilled from his tiny eye lenses, and the egg-shaped duel avatar shouted, "I like Choco, too...And Crow... So I want to fight! I want to fight lots more. I want to get strong and be friends!!"

"...Avo..." Magenta Scissor called her partner's name in a stifled voice, and the tension drained from her body bit by bit. Pulling her hand away from her knife, she gently stroked Avocado's armor. When she lifted her face and looked at Shihoko, she asked, the anger in her voice faded, "Chocolat Puppeter, you... What do you want from us?"

"I want you," Shihoko said, placing her other hand over the one on her chest, "to fight the Acceleration Research Society with us—with Nega Nebulus."

# 10

"You damned bird—I mean, you damned Silver Crow!!" the skull-faced rider yelled, straddling the large American motorcycle and thrusting out a tightly clenched fist. "Today, for sure, I'm putting our fighting to The End!!"

"That's just what I was hoping for, Ash—I mean, Ash Roller!!" Haruyuki thrust his own fist up as he waited for the motorcycle charging forward, exhaust jetting from the muffler. "Let's finish this...On this day, the end of the first term!!"

Saturday, July 20, 2047. 7:50 AM. Once again, the regular Ash-Crow battle was taking place on Ring Road No. 7, which cut north-south through Suginami Area No. 3.

That afternoon was the Legion merger meeting with Prominence, and that evening was the long-awaited trip to Minato Ward Area No. 3; it was an important day with the decisive battle with Oscillatory Universe ahead. Haruyuki thought he should maybe take at least today off from his regular duel with Ash Roller and save his energy, but they couldn't allow the Oscillatory side to get wind of the Territories' attack by some chance. Given that, he decided he should avoid doing anything different from usual, and so Haruyuki had accepted Ash's challenge.

Once the duel started, the time flew by, and in the remaining five minutes, both of their health gauges had just 10 percent left.

Whoever could deal some serious damage in this charge would be the winner. That said, they had both used up their special-attack gauges, so they could only use regular attacks. And Ash had the advantage there with his V-twin Punch, a special technique he had developed himself.

"Here we goooooooo!!" Ash howled, racing furiously along the cracked main thoroughfare of the Century End stage. "Super! Special! Max V-twin Puuuuuuuuuunch!! Towaaaaah!!" He jumped and stood up on the bike, setting his right foot on the throttle and his left on the tandem seat to ride the metal horse like a surfer.

Once he was about thirty meters from Haruyuki, he used his toes to deftly operate the front brake for an instantaneous full-lock turn. At the same time, he made the back tire power-slide and spun the bike sideways at top speed. Carving out a spiral of flames on the road, he became a mass of kinetic energy to assault Haruyuki.

The instant the double-spinning tire touched him, the remainder of Haruyuki's health gauge would definitely be knocked flying. The last time he'd had this serious trick used on him, he'd tried to dodge by jumping straight up into the air, but Ash had responded with a wild technique called a Jackknife Guillotine, a handstand with the bike in the spinning state. The rear tire had grazed his stomach and taken over 10 percent of his gauge, so he couldn't dodge like that again here. Still, if he tried to jump to either side, the bike would have no problems chasing after him.

"Whoa! So this is the end?!"

"A crow that can't fly's just a plain old crow!!"

"Can't a plain old crow fly, though?"

Listening to the voices from the Gallery coming down on them from the buildings on either side of the road, Haruyuki thought hard: *Forward's obviously out of the question. Up/down's out; the sides are out. So then, the only direction left is back. But running around dodging until time runs out so I can get a draw isn't exactly the greatest end to the First-Term Final Ash-Crow Fight.*

*No. I keep getting stuck because I'm only thinking about running.*

*Tight spots are exactly when you hold your ground, go forward. That's what Kuroyukihime and Fuko would do.*

"Go!!" Haruyuki focused on only the motorcycle transformed into a spinning, flaming top charging toward him and kicked off the ground. Not forward nor up nor sideways nor backward; diagonally forward, to the right.

"You're out, you're out, you're abooooooout!!" Ash corrected the trajectory of his charge. Spinning to the left, he turned left and closed in, trying to knock Haruyuki into next week.

"Hngraaaaaaah!" Feeling the scattering sparks bouncing off him, Haruyuki ran with everything he had. To the left to match the bike's spin, ever left. His special-attack gauge was empty, so he couldn't fly, but he used his spread wings as a rudder and ran, ran, ran, carving out a circle.

"Nyaaaaaah! Tera poweeeeerrrrr!" Ash opened the throttle all the way, and the V-twin engine roared as the speed of the motorcycle's spinning increased.

Haruyuki kept dashing around it at unprecedented speed.

*Faster...Faster!!* As he prayed, Silver Crow moved more and more quickly, particles of light shooting from the armor of his white-hot feet. Eventually, a white circle with a radius of seven meters was beaten into the surface of the road, combining with the red flames jetting from the rear tire of the motorcycle to create overlapping dual rings.

*Now that I'm thinking about it, it's been ages since I ran so seriously like this in a normal duel,* Haruyuki suddenly thought, even as he sensed the moment of decision approaching. Lately, he'd been so totally focused on his flying speed that he'd stopped thinking about movement on the ground, a duel fundamental. Even still, at some point, Silver Crow had become extremely fleet of foot.

*How about I stop pursuing speed, trying to borrow the system's power? Can't I just look for that in my own heart—in the naked body of my duel avatar?*

"Ah...Aaaaaaaaaah!!" Letting out a battle cry, Haruyuki pushed himself to run another step faster.

The instant that Silver Crow's running speed surpassed the spinning speed of Ash Roller, the bike's front fork—on the receiving end of a massive amount of power for so long—snapped in half. The engine plunged into the ground, followed by a massive explosion.

Blown back by the flames, Ash Roller shot up toward the night sky. "Our fight!! Starts now!! Eternaaaaaaaal!!"

And then he blew up like fireworks, flashy particles exploding everywhere.

Once the duel was over, and he woke up on the pedestrian bridge that cut across Ring Road No. 7, Haruyuki stayed where he was to wait for the bus that Ash Roller's "real self" was probably on.

A minute or so later, an EV bus running southward stopped at the bus stop below him, and several passengers got on before it quietly pulled away again. He started to turn around to see the bus off as it slipped under the bridge, but then he noticed a lone figure remaining at the bus stop after the bus had left, and he hurriedly turned on his heel.

A girl in uniform, short-sleeved blouse with a skirt with the same checked pattern, was waving at him. He didn't need to see the slightly wavy short hair to know that this was the younger sister of the Century End rider he'd been fighting a few minutes earlier, Rin Kusakabe. She stopped him with both hands when he tried to come down from the pedestrian bridge and raced up the stairs, a shining smile on her face as she dipped her head toward him. "Good morning, Arita."

"'Morning, Kusakabe," Haruyuki returned the greeting and then cocked his head to one side. "What's going on?"

"Right…Uh. Um," Rin mumbled as she checked the time and then said with an apologetic expression, "I'm sorry to. Bother you before. School…Could we. Talk. A minute?"

"Y-yeah, of course," he replied, hurriedly looking around. There weren't that many, but there were still some people on the pedestrian bridge, so it wasn't really the best place for confidential conversation. Or so he thought.

"I'm sorry," she said in a small voice. "I have to get on the. Bus that's coming in ten minutes, so here…" Rin pulled a small disk-shaped object out of her school bag. He stared, wondering what it was for a second, until he finally realized it was an XSB cable cord reel.

"Huh? But. Um…," Haruyuki stammered, while Rin pulled a small plug from the reel and inserted it into her Neurolinker. With a red face, she offered the other plug to Haruyuki.

A girl and a boy directing in a public space were dating; the shorter the cable, the closer they were—these customs were said to be "unenlightened" among the type of adults who worked hard with the latest Neurolinker models. But in junior high and high school culture, they were still very current. He had to wonder, though, what the cord-reel type meant, when it could change from a maximum length of one meter to a minimum of fifty centimeters. With these thoughts in his mind, Haruyuki connected the plug to his Neurolinker.

The wired connection warning had no sooner disappeared than Rin's neurospeak voice was echoing in his mind.

*"Um, I'm sorry. In a place like this…I have something. Important to discuss. Though."*

*"U-uh-uh, I'm totally…"* Fine with it? He wasn't sure if he could really say that, so he let his sentence fade out.

Rin smiled a little and put just a bit of distance between them. The pastel-green cord reel that hung between them sparkled in the light of the summer morning.

*"S-so what's the important thing?"* he asked, his heart pounding a little belatedly.

*"The truth is…"* Rin stared directly at him as she made him hear her voice, with an increased note of seriousness. *"I have. A message for you from…My brother…"*

*"A-a message?! From Ash?!"* He very nearly cried out in his real voice and hurried to purse his lips shut tight as he muttered in his mind, *"He could've just told me himself in the duel before, though."*

*"He said it's…giga embarrassing."*

*"…I-it is? So then, what's the message?"* Haruyuki asked.

Rin gently stroked the Neurolinker on her neck with one hand. This Neurolinker, metallic-gray shell with a lightning-bolt crack running across it, was not originally hers. It belonged to her older brother, Rinta Kusakabe, who had been in a coma in a hospital in Shibuya for the last two years after a motorcycle race accident.

Through whatever logic, Rin could dive into the Accelerated World as the Burst Linker Ash Roller only when she was wearing her brother's Neurolinker. While accelerated, her brother Rinta fought—for Rin, it apparently felt like she was watching over the fight from the tandem seat of the motorcycle—but it wasn't clear if that was actually Rinta's spirit being transferred from the hospital or just a second personality within Rin called Rinta.

The one thing that *was* certain was that Ash/Rinta adored Rin and would explode in anger if Haruyuki got too close to—or too distant from—her. Ash would definitely remember today's directing and have a few choice words for Haruyuki in their next duel. Although Haruyuki and Rin were both off for summer holidays starting the following day, so there wouldn't be the Tuesday-Thursday-Saturday Ash-Crow fight for a while.

His thoughts had made it that far when he suddenly realized something. *"I-is Ash's message maybe about summer vacation? Does he want to decide a day and time and keep having regular fights?"*

*"No, it's not— Oh! I'd be happy if. You did that. Though…Oh! No, it's not that."* Faint color rising up in her cheeks once more, Rin shook her head and pulled herself back together. *"The message. Is about…today's. Territories."*

*"……!!"*

Haruyuki's eyes flew wide open. Ash Roller had taken part in the mock Territories with the Green Legion the previous Sunday. Thus, he knew about Nega Nebulus's planned attack on Minato Area No. 3, but even so, what on earth would he have to say on the very day of the attack?

*"Wh-what's Ash say?"*

"*Um.*" Stammering for a moment, or rather letting her neuro-speak lapse, Rin closed the distance between them another five centimeters. Her untucked blouse flapped, and a sweet smell came wafting up. Naturally, Haruyuki couldn't help but get flustered, but the next words she said knocked even this feeling out of his heart. "*Um, my brother. Says he wants. To be at the Legion meeting before the Territories.*"

"*Huh?*"

"*Actually, it's not just him…U and Oli, too…*"

"*Whaaat?!*"

The Legion meeting—did he mean the meeting about the merger with Prominence? Reeling, he saw the brave figures of the Rough Valley Rollers, the three-person team of Ash Roller, Bush Utan, and Olive Grab, in the back of his mind.

Once the closing ceremony ended before lunch that day, all the Legion members, including Fuko, Utai, and Chocolat's gang, were meeting at Haruyuki's house. Fortunately, the kendo team was also just having a meeting today, given that the meet was the following day, so Takumu would be able to join up with them around one. They were going to have lunch together, and then at two o'clock, the merger meeting with Prominence would finally start.

They would move to Nakano Central Park, the large commercial facility near the border between Prominence territory, Nakano Area No. 1, and Nega Nebulus territory, Suginami Area No. 1, with their global connections off and then connect using only the local net inside the mall. After first checking the matching list and confirming that there were no Burst Linkers other than the attending members from both sides—which had been agreed upon in advance—they would begin the duel with Sky Raker and Blood Leopard as the starters while the rest of the attendees would dive as members of the Gallery. So it would have been possible to have Rin and the others take part if they came to the mall, but if Nega Nebulus requested additional attendees at this point—and members of Great Wall on top of that—the Prominence side would no doubt be alarmed and on guard.

And then Haruyuki had a sudden realization. *"Um, what meeting does Ash want to come to?"*

*"Uh. The Nega Nebulus meeting. Before the Territories."*

*"Th-that one, huh…?"* The tension drained from his shoulders, and Rin blinked with a curious expression. Now that he thought about it, there's no way Rin or Ash would know anything about the Legion merger when they'd only decided on it yesterday. *"Sorry, sorry. I was thinking of something else. Uh, so that meeting, we don't do it full dive or in a duel stage. It's in the real."*

*"Oh. Then. It will be difficult. To attend."* Rin dropped her head.

*"Um, if it's just you, I think it'll be okay,"* Haruyuki hurried to add. *"You've already met everyone a bunch of times."*

*"Thank you, Arita. But if it's just me, that might not. Achieve my brother's objective."*

*"It won't, huh? …What's his objective?"* Haruyuki asked casually, but what Rin said next after a slight hesitation was so shocking that if they had been in the Accelerated World, he probably would've jumped a meter or so in surprise, flown over the pedestrian bridge guardrail, and fell onto the road headfirst.

*"My brother…to participate in today's Territories. With U and Oli… he wants to leave. Great Wall temporarily and join Nega Nebulus."*

"Whaaaaaaaat?!"

Haruyuki shrieked in his real voice, and a passing businessman turned a doubtful eye on him.

The closing ceremony started at nine that morning, and he sat through first opening remarks from the vice principal, then a speech by the principal, the presentation of club and team awards, an activity report from the student council, several warnings about summer vacation, and the closing remarks from the vice principal. The whole thing was over at 9:50. Chiyuri and Takumu both received certificates at the podium for their various meets—just certificates, although they were real paper—and Haruyuki clapped for them with his heart and soul.

After that, there was an extended homeroom in each classroom, and their homeroom teacher, Sugano, handed out report cards. This was digital data, and he'd always need a fair bit of mental strength to bring himself to click on it, but his test results that term had been all right, so he was able to open the file without having to brace himself too much.

His assessment in every subject except gym was much improved, but what made Haruyuki happy were the comments in the remarks column about his work with the Animal Care Club. Resolving anew to take good care of Hoo over summer vacation, he closed the report card window and listened impatiently to his teacher's usual lecture on how summer vacation was a critical period for eighth graders blah blah blah.

This rambling speech kept going right up until the last second of long homeroom until, finally, their teacher Sugano wrapped up with the slight pressure of "Okay then, show me your smiling faces in the second term!" The bell rang, and the instant the teacher vanished out the door, an atmosphere of liberation filled the classroom.

Listening to the joyful chatter of his classmates and the clattering of chairs, Haruyuki stayed in his own seat, took a deep breath, and slowly exhaled it.

The first term of eighth grade really had been eventful. In April, Seiji Nomi, aka Dusk Taker, a new student a grade below Haruyuki, suddenly showed up to plunge Haruyuki into a desperate adversity both in the Accelerated World and the real world. At the time, the future had seemed closed off by darkness, but with the help of Niko, Fuko, Chiyuri, Takumu, and Kuroyukihime, he had just barely won the difficult battle against Nomi.

At the beginning of June, there'd been the Hermes' Cord race, and after the tumult of the race event, Fuko had returned to the Legion.

In the middle of June, still riding on that momentum or perhaps on the spur of the moment, he had stood as a candidate for a member of the Animal Care Club. He'd wondered what would happen to him when he ended up taking over as president, but thanks to that, he'd been able to meet Hoo and Utai. He and his friends had charged the Castle to rescue Utai from a state of Unlimited EK, and inside the Castle, he'd encountered Trilead Tetroxide there and made the promise to meet again.

After that, he'd turned into the sixth Chrome Disaster in the middle of the ISS kit incident, but thanks to Rin Kusakabe intently putting herself in his way to pull him back, he'd returned to his own self. The curse of the Armor of Catastrophe had been undone by Utai's purification ability, and they'd sealed The Destiny and Star Caster away from the world.

At the end of June, he'd met Wolfram Cerberus and Chocolat Puppeter and her friends, and on the day of the school festival at the end of the month, they'd had one mission after another—the rescue of Aqua Current, the attack on the Archangel Metatron, and the return of Niko, who'd been abducted to the Acceleration Research Society's headquarters. Just before the end of the school festival, the White King had appeared and admitted that she was the president of the Acceleration Research Society, bringing one act to a close.

Even after the start of July, he'd been invited by Mayu Ikuzawa to run for student council election; there'd been the mock Territories with the Green Legion; the last of the Four Elements, Graphite Edge, had reappeared; the three members of Petit Paquet had joined Nega Nebulus—all kinds of things had happened. Two days earlier, Haruyuki had broken into the Castle again with Fuko and been reunited with Trilead. When they got home, Niko and Pard had told them about the Legion merger. And now today, they would finally have their decisive battle with the White Legion, Oscillatory Universe.

Well, as decisive as it was in his mind, in terms of the Brain Burst system, it would be no different from the normal Territories. So even if in the worst case, they were defeated, or he was pushed to total point loss, that wouldn't spell the annihilation of the Legion. But they wouldn't be able to use this trick again—stealing the White Legion's right to block the matching list and pull back the cover on the Acceleration Research Society. The Society had cultivated the Armor of Catastrophe, Mark II, which housed Cerberus, with the Invincible part they stole from Niko, and they would no doubt bring about in the Accelerated World a new—and far greater—catastrophe than the ISS kits.

The Territories would certainly be a much fiercer battle than any before. But they had to win. For Niko's sake, for Cerberus's sake...and for the sake of all the Burst Linkers who had helped and guided Haruyuki up to that point.

"...ta. Arita."

Feeling a tap-tap on his shoulder, Haruyuki opened his eyes in surprise.

Standing there was Mayu Ikuzawa, all ready to go home. When she met Haruyuki's eyes, she giggled and bent over to murmur, "I'll probably mail you a bunch of stuff about the election over summer break, so please and thank you."

"Oh y-yeah, of course."

"'Kay, see you!" She headed off in a trot.

"Yeah. S-see you." He watched her slip out the door.

"And what was *that*?"

The voice came down upon him from behind, and he turned around nervously to find Chiyuri, also finished packing up to leave. She looked down on him suspiciously, and he unconsciously replied, "N-not that."

"What's 'not that'?"

"Oh. Uh. That was just official stuff...like logistics...Anyway, uh, where's Taku?"

"He already went to practice. He said he'll come straight to your place when the meeting's over."

"Oh, o-okay." He bobbed his head up and down and then stood up to pack his things. The time was 11:40 AM. The Legion members were meeting at the Arita house at noon, so if he didn't head home soon, he wouldn't make it in time. "O-okay, let's hurry, Chiyu!"

"Now look! *You* were the one doing logistics or ballistics or whatever with the class rep!"

"Whoa! Look at the time!"

"Come on! Don't try to slip out of this!"

They stepped out of the classroom, and when he changed into his sneakers at the shoe lockers, he tried to step toward the entrance, but Chiyuri yanked on his collar.

"Hey! You're forgetting your indoor shoes!"

"Ah...O-oh, right." He put his shoes in the plastic bag he'd brought for that purpose, shoved it into his school bag, and jumped outside.

The burning sunlight of midsummer poured down from the pure-blue sky and burned his eyes.

# 11

Kuroyukihime—Black Lotus
Fuko Kurasaki—Sky Raker
Utai Shinomiya—Ardor Maiden
Akira Himi—Aqua Current
Chiyuri Kurashima—Lime Bell
Shihoko Nago—Chocolat Puppeter
Satomi Mito—Mint Mitten
Yume Yuruki—Plum Flipper
Rin Kusakabe—Ash Roller

These nine girls were supposed to be the only attendees of the real meeting/dinner party that started at noon, with Takumu joining them later. However, Haruyuki, hectic with welcoming one girl after another, suddenly noticed an anomaly once they were all finally settled in the living room.

As people got carried away chatting on the sofa set and at the dining table, he started counting them on his fingers from where he stood in the entrance to the kitchen. "One, two, three..." And then again. And then one more time still.

"......?!"

He very nearly screamed but then clamped both hands over his mouth. *There are ten people!!*

He was sure of it. Five directly in front of him. Five on the balcony side. He pulled back into the kitchen and listed up everyone in his mind to see if he'd somehow forgotten one of their number, but no matter how he racked his memory, he could only come up with nine people.

Then the voice of Chocolat Puppeter—Shihoko Nago—rang out from the living room. "I'll bring more tea, okay?!"

Her footsteps preceded her, and then the girl herself appeared in the kitchen. He had no sooner met her eyes than he was quickly beckoning her with one hand. She approached with a curious expression.

"Choco, this is bad," he whispered. "There are ten people!"

"Huh? What does that matter?"

"There should only be nine! The extra person has to be some kind of social engineering thing from another Legion!"

"Social—" She raised an eyebrow. "What's that, Crow?"

"Um, like hackers and crackers making direct contact with a target in the real world and taking their info— No, no, this is not the time to talk about that." He shook his head from side to side.

"Huh?" Shihoko frowned with sudden realization. The hair tied on both sides of her head swung as she whispered, "Weird. Didn't Kuroyuki tell you?"

"Huh? What?"

"I called her last night, though."

"Uh? What?" Haruyuki leaned forward, but before Shihoko could answer, Kuroyukihime called from the living room.

"Haruyuki, come here a moment!"

"Oh…Um…O-okay…" Unable to say no, he nervously stepped out of the kitchen and moved forward at a snail's pace, his guard up.

"Sorry for not telling you." Kuroyukihime smiled mischievously. "I just wondered when you'd notice. The truth is I came with a secret guest."

"A-a guest?" Relaxing now that it seemed like no hostile covert operator had gotten the jump on them, he moved to a spot beside Kuroyukihime on the sofa and checked the faces of the girls' squad in turn. And found that there was indeed one face he didn't know, seated in between Chiyuri and Satomi Mito.

From the look of her, she was older—maybe in the same grade as Fuko. Her pale-blue, short-sleeved sailor-style uniform was a design he'd never seen before. Her longish front bangs were cut asymmetrically, and a fairly mysterious air hung around her. There was no smile on her pale lips.

"Uh. Um." Haruyuki dipped his head, feeling a little pressure. "It's nice to meet you. I'm Nega Nebulus's Haruyuki Arita— Oh! My avatar name is Silver Crow."

The girl in the sailor uniform returned the bow, her diagonal bangs shifting, and gave her own name in a husky voice that suited her very well. "Hello, Silver Crow. I'm Rui Odagiri."

"Odagiri…" He'd never heard the name before, either. But he felt like he'd met her somewhere before and furrowed his brow. This sense of déjà vu exploded into tiny pieces the instant she spoke again.

"My avatar name is Magenta Scissor."

"………"

"Whaaaaa—?!" Haruyuki shrieked and started to fall over, but anticipating this reaction, Kuroyukihime held him up with a hand and set him on his feet once more. He turned back to her and cried, flapping his hands, "K-Ku-Kuroyukihi—! M—! M-Ma-Magmagmag—"

"Mmm. Speaking of magic, mixed rice is always such a neat trick. Might be nice for lunch," Kuroyukihime said.

"Sounds good," Fuko agreed. "*Myoga*, edamame, perilla leaves, very summery."

"Oh! That sounds yummy! Let's shred some fish and throw that in, too!" Chiyuri raised her hand.

UI> AND NOW IT SEEMS THAT I'M HUNGRY came the comment from Utai, and by this time, Haruyuki had finally succeeded in rebooting his brain.

"M-Maga-Coba—I mean, Magenta, what are you doing here?!" he shouted once more.

Finally, the girl who had given her name as Rui Odagiri moved her mouth, the corners climbing into a coquettish smile, something she did indeed share with the scissor-wielding avatar. "Your character is exactly the same as it is over there, hmm, Silver Crow?"

"Ah…Uh, i-is it?"

"The reason I'm visiting you today is because Choco and the girls scouted me."

"Oh. I-is that what happened? …But like, wait. S-scouted?!" He whirled around to stare at Shihoko, who had emerged from the kitchen.

Shihoko, who had previously fought fierce battles against Magenta, laughed sheepishly when she met Haruyuki's eyes.

"Um, well, not to get ahead of things here, but we went to Setagaya Number Five to see Magenta and ask her to come fight with us," Yume, formerly the brains of the Petit Paquet organization, announced as she looked over the frame of her glasses. "There was a bunch of stuff in the middle there, but that's how it turned out."

"Hey, heeeey!" Shihoko shouted, running over to give Yume a chop on the head.

"Ouch!"

"C'mon, Yume! Don't skip the important bits! I tried super-hard out there!"

"……?"

Haruyuki cocked his head to one side curiously, and Magenta/Rui smiled.

"Choco challenged Avo and me all by herself when we were tag teaming and got a win by decision."

"W-wow!" He could only be obediently surprised at this. Chocolat Puppeter was level five while Magenta Scissor was six, and Avocado Avoider was also five. A solo victory over a tag team with an added-together level of double hers was nothing other than a truly spectacular achievement.

But Shihoko laughed with embarrassment once more as she shook her head. "Uh-uh. The truth is, I just fought Avocado one-on-one. But I feel like that was the first time I've worked so hard in a solo duel."

"You did...So wait. Avocado isn't here...?" Haruyuki shifted his gaze from Shihoko.

"Unfortunately, Avo can't move away from Setagaya," Rui replied, shaking her lustrous black hair. "He's been in the hospital for a long time now."

"Hospital...," Haruyuki murmured.

Rui glanced at him before turning to Satomi next to her. "I think you would know it, Mint. There's that big hospital right next to Kinuta Park, right?"

"Oh. Right." Satomi nodded. "The place where they treat children."

"Right. Originally, it was called the National Children's Hospital, but now it's the National Center for Child Health and Development. That's where Avo and I met," Magenta Scissor said.

Utai began to move her fingers quickly. UI> I WENT MYSELF A NUMBER OF TIMES FOR TESTS FOR APHASIA.

"So then, maybe I just missed you there, Maiden," Rui replied, a faint smile crossing her lips, and then continued. "Avo's disease isn't the life-threatening kind. But I can't actually be the one to tell you what it is. He's really dying to meet all the Nega Nebulus members, so I'd love it if you'd come to Setagaya Five at some point."

"Yes. Of course. At the time, we'll invite him to join the Legion as well," Kuroyukihime replied, and Rui dipped her head in thanks.

Staring at all this, Haruyuki absolutely couldn't help but think that the fact that they met in the hospital meant that Rui, too, had a reason for getting treatment or being hospitalized there.

As if reading his mind, Rui turned her gaze on him. The diagonal cut of her bangs almost completely covered her right eye, so that only her left eye shone with a strong light. Smiling once again, she parted her lips. "A few years ago, a small-scale Legion was born at the National Center for Child Health and

Development. More than a few kids hospitalized or getting treatment there had had to wear a Neurolinker since soon after they were born because of their illnesses. I did, too."

She cut herself off there for a moment and looked down at her own hands.

"I have what's called Gertsmann syndrome. My own symptoms are finger agnosia and left-right disorientation. So basically, I have a hard time distinguishing my own fingers, and I don't understand left or right. With my Neurolinker, I can display a mark on my fingers and hands, but even so, I've had the thought a million times: Just one hand would be fine; just one finger would be good—and yet."

Haruyuki looked at Rui's slender hands and then suddenly noticed that her right wrist was encircled by a zigzagging scar. It was almost like she had tried to cut off her hand with a large pair of scissors.

"You said that you hate pairs of things that are one, Magenta… Is that why?" Unconsciously, Haruyuki gave voice to this question. In his heart, he panicked that he'd gone and asked something rude, but the look on Rui's face didn't change as she nodded.

"There's that, too. Chopsticks, shoes, scissors…And human arms create a left-right just by existing there. I mean, when I was taught how to use chopsticks at daycare, I was told to put the right chopstick between the index finger and thumb, middle finger of my right hand—and the left chopstick between my thumb and middle finger, ring finger…Just hearing that, I thought I'd lose my mind."

Chuckling, she laid her hands in her lap and continued quietly.

"So when I got Brain Burst from a kid I knew at the hospital, and my own duel avatar had arms and fingers like normal, I was a little disappointed. But…the most disappointing thing was that the Burst Linkers besides me picked on Avo, who was the last to join us, because of his appearance. I thought, well, this is just the same as the outside world. But I didn't have the power to stop them; they were all higher level than me. So I got ahold of the ISS kits...and drove all the Burst Linkers at the treatment center to total point loss, including my parent and Avo's."

The entire group listened silently to Rui's monologue. The internal strife and collapse of a small-scale community was absolutely not unheard of in the Accelerated World. But she hadn't simply let the situation unfold; she'd sought power of her own will and used it.

"I don't regret doing that. But...you all surpassed the power of the ISS kit, when I thought they could change the Accelerated World. So I want to keep an eye on your fight until the end. And if you'll permit me, I'd like to fight again, alongside you this time. Of course...that is if you'll have me after I did those things..."

Even after Rui closed her mouth, no one moved to say anything for a while.

Haruyuki slowly looked over at Rin, seated the furthest away from Rui at one end of the dining table. Her older brother Ash Roller had been forcibly parasitized with an ISS kit at Magenta Scissor's hand the day before the school festival last month. In order to save Rin suffering from the mental interference from the kit, Ash had been prepared to even be banished from the Accelerated World with the Judgment Blow.

Before the mental interference could become that serious, however, they had managed to destroy the main kit body, albeit with some difficulty, but there was no doubt that it had been rough on Rin and Ash. How would Rin take what Magenta Scissor was saying here?

Then Rin lifted her head finally, having kept it down all this time, and looked at Haruyuki. Her usual gentle smile rose up on her face, and she nodded slowly before turning and taking a deep breath.

"Taking an 'over' thing and making it a 'forever' thing is basic 'nothiiiiiing'!!"

Her sudden shout made everyone present jump. Rin, her cheeks colored with embarrassment, shrank back into herself and continued in a thin voice, "...Is what my brother would say. I think. It's true my brother. Ash Roller. Did fight Magenta Scissor and was forced to equip the ISS kit. But I think he felt. Something through the parallel. Circuits of the ISS kit. The feelings of the ones who. Sought the ISS kit power themselves. Utan, Olive... and Magenta Scissor and them."

Rui Odagiri didn't know the mysterious connection between Ash Roller and Rin Kusakabe, but she lowered her face without asking a single question. She looked down at her right hand with its faint scars and gently closed her fingers.

"If you have ten Burst Linkers, you have ten ways to be right," Kuroyukihime suddenly said in a resolute voice. "My master, Graphite Edge, always used to say that. At the time, I simply thought he was putting on airs again and let it go in one ear and out the other...But now, I think that might actually be the case. It goes without saying that my 'right,' aiming as I am for level ten, is nothing other than 'wrong' to the other kings...And the actions of the White King and the Acceleration Research Society, which we believe to be wrong, are perhaps unshakeably just to them. Yes...That's why I have no intention of judging what you did as evil, Magenta Scissor. And all the more so if it was something you did not for your own profit, but for the sake of so many Burst Linkers."

Hearing this, Rui bit her bottom lip hard. She closed her eyes, and a small valley was carved in between her eyebrows. She stayed like that for about three seconds, but then the tension quickly drained out of her body. Her face had the same cool expression—no, the light of a powerful will that hadn't been there before shone in her left eye as she turned her whole body toward Kuroyukihime.

"Black King...Black Lotus. I want you to forgive me and let Avocado Avoider and me fight with you as Legion members." Her head lowered, she raised her hands, and after what looked like a moment's hesitation, she pushed her two hands out in front of her.

"I cannot forgive you," Kuroyukihime announced quietly. "Because neither I nor my comrades have a single reason for you to seek forgiveness from us. In fact, we would gladly have you, Magenta Scissor. I would be delighted to have someone as dependable as you join our Legion as a comrade before the large battle we face."

She smiled once more and took Rui's hands with her own, gripping them tightly.

Head still lowered, her long bangs hung forward to obscure Rui's face, but even so, Haruyuki could see that her thin lips were pursed like she was holding something back. Haruyuki felt certain at least that whatever it was, it wasn't anger or sadness.

Once the Legion membership procedures were taken care of through a normal duel between Kuroyukihime and Rui Odagiri via the Arita home net—he wasn't sure if it was a relief or a regret that there was no actual fighting in order to conserve their strength—the entire party got to work on lunch.

With the ten girls and one boy, and then Takumu joining them at one for a total of twelve people, it was their largest dinner table so far.

"There's a ton of frozen pizza," Haruyuki proposed in earnest.

But Chiyuri immediately rejected that idea. "Now look, I'm totally in the mood for mixed rice now!"

"Y-you are…But I mean, just rice…"

"Well, that's true." She thought for a second. "If we make *onigiri* out of the mixed rice, then we're fine with another side dish and some kind of soup. I mean, it is just lunch. Ui, what do you think would be good?"

UI> Let's see. For the soup, how about a summery Japanese-style broad bean potage?

"Oooh, the elementary kids these days know some stylish recipeeees!" Chiyuri caught Utai from behind and pinched her cheeks with both hands.

UI> Plse stp tha

"But what about the other dish?" she asked, and a voice came from somewhere surprising.

"*Karaage.*"

"Huh?" He looked over at the speaker.

Akira, the bouncer, had maintained her silence during the meeting, but now she repeated with an extremely serious expression, "*Karaage* goes with *onigiri.*"

The rest could only nod wordlessly.

Since the menu was set, Haruyuki accepted the position of grocery squad leader and hurried down to the food sales area of the mall. With the power of the Kuroyukihime-made shopping efficiency improvement app, he cleared the large shopping list in a mere five minutes and managed to get a butterfly point while he was at it before returning to his house.

After that, he had basically nothing to do. Plus, there were ten girls crowded into the living/dining/kitchen area of the Arita house. He shelled broad beans as he shivered at the thought of what would happen if his mother was to come home for some reason.

At any rate, they had the personnel if nothing else, so at basically the same time that Takumu rang the doorbell at one o'clock, lunch was set out on the table: shredded mackerel, edamame, *myoga*, and perilla mixed-rice *onigiri*; chilled broad bean and soy milk Japanese-style potage; and a mountain of chicken *karaage*.

Stepping into the living room behind Haruyuki, Takumu set eyes on the crowd of girls and the pile of *karaage* and froze in place. "Haru, what is this…? I can't even believe it's real…"

"It's too soon for freaking out, Taku," Haruyuki whispered back, beckoning Rui Odagiri with one hand. When Rui and Takumu were facing each other, he cleared his throat and raised his right hand. "Um, Odagiri, this is Takumu Mayuzumi—Cyan Pile."

"Hello. I'm glad we can meet in the real." The usual Magenta smile crept onto Rui's lips, and Takumu returned her bow with a doubtful look.

Haruyuki cleared his throat once again and raised his left hand. "And, Taku, this is our new Legion member Rui Odagiri—Magenta Scissor."

"It's a pleasure to—" After extending his right hand, Takumu reeled for once, as he uttered the strange sound, "*Majenza*?!"

With an unprecedented twelve people at the historic and traditional Nega Nebulus dinner party, Chef Chiyuri and Sous-chef Utai had intended to make more than enough food, but the *onigiri*, potage, and *karaage* vanished completely in twenty minutes.

But that wasn't to say there wasn't enough food; everyone thanked them for the meal with satisfied faces before they stood to clean up. Once they were done with that, the clock read one thirty PM. The group then gathered in the living room, and Legion Master Kuroyukihime and Submaster Fuko stood with their backs to the balcony.

"First, I'll just confirm," Kuroyukihime began. "May I assume that all the members who go to schools other than Umesato also had the closing ceremony for the first term today?"

Fuko, Utai, Rui, Rin, and Akira all nodded, while Shihoko, the representative for a group of three, chimed in, "You may!"

"Mmm. Well then, that means that everyone here is on summer break starting tomorrow. I'm sure you all have exciting plans. Of course, I do as well."

Here, she turned her gaze toward Haruyuki momentarily, so he replied with the thought *I'm excited about the trip to Yamagata, too!* He wasn't certain whether that got through to her or not, but she did smile faintly before continuing her speech.

"And in order to make this summer break fun and full, we absolutely cannot lose against Oscillatory Universe in the Territories today. Unfortunately, I must remain behind to defend Suginami area, but we have even more trustworthy comrades now, and I firmly believe you will achieve our objective. Please. I'm counting on you." Kuroyukihime bowed her head.

Fuko thrust her fist high into the air. "Everyone, let's fight as hard as we can so we can report victory to Sacchi!"

"Yaaaah!!" the ten cried in unison, the sound filling the large living room.

1:40 PM.

Nega Nebulus, with a current roster of eleven people—twelve with the Archangel Metatron—formed a group with Rin Kusakabe, who still belonged to Great Wall in terms of the system, and sallied forth from the Arita house. However, they didn't dive into the Unlimited Neutral Field like they had on previous missions. They lined up in the entryway, put on their shoes, and filed into the condo hallway in pairs.

Their first destination was the mixed-use commercial facility Nakano Central Park near JR Nakano Station. This was just over a kilometer away, but even on foot, they could reach it in fifteen minutes.

As Haruyuki walked alongside Takumu at the tail end of the group, his childhood friend said to him in a low voice, "Haru, it might be time to seriously think about the extreme imbalance in the ratio of boys and girls in our Legion."

"Agreed on all fronts," Haruyuki answered, while girls in a rich variation of six different kinds of uniforms—Akira only was in her usual jeans—led them, looking dashing as they walked. They looked so much like they were out of a movie, and Haruyuki had to confess that he would have been lying if he said he had absolutely no desire to record them.

"Oh, but it might improve a bit soon," he murmured, tugging on the sleeve of Rin Kusakabe walking immediately ahead of them. When Rin looked back, he peeled her away from the rest of the girls' squad and asked in a low voice, "Um, Kusakabe. Will Utan and Olive be okay?"

"Oh. Yes. They're already. On standby somewhere in. Nakano One."

"They are? Okay, then all that's left is the joining procedures."

Listening to this conversation, Takumu cocked his head to the side, curious. Haruyuki simply said to that "I'll explain later" and let his thoughts race for a moment.

Kuroyukihime had already been informed of the application to join Nega Nebulus from the three-person group of Ash, Utan, and Olive. To be more precise, what they wanted was a limited transfer until the fight with the Acceleration Research Society was settled, but Kuroyukihime had assented without hesitation. No matter how much power they had, it could never be too much, and there was no need to consider the possibility of Ash and the others being spies.

"Come to think of it, in the space of a week, we've gotten loads more comrades, huh?" Haruyuki said, half to himself, as they waited for the elevator.

The three members of Petit Paquet. Magenta Scissor and Avocado Avoider—although he wasn't yet a member. Ash and his two friends. Adding in Metatron, they were a total of sixteen. Plus, Haruyuki was waiting on a message from one more person, more reliable than anyone else.

And in less than an hour, Nega Nebulus would take on the negotiations for a merger with Prominence. If everything went according to plan, a new Legion with nearly fifty members would be born in an instant, a fighting force that didn't pale in the slightest in comparison with the Legions of the other Kings.

Of course, he was anxious about the Legion growing. Would the suddenly large organization be able to come together as one? Would differences of opinions invite their split again?

*No. What I'm really afraid of is losing the Nega Nebulus of now, the cozy and comfortable Nega Nebulus. Of being buried among Burst Linkers with higher levels, more skills, of Silver Crow losing this place where he belongs. It's an entirely egotistical, selfish anxiety. But I can't deny that I do have these feelings in one corner of my heart.*

"Haru."

Abruptly, Takumu's voice descended near his ear.

"Nega Nebulus at first was just you and Master, and you're the reason it's gotten so big now. You kept trying your hardest, and now this many people have come together under the black flag. I'm no exception, either."

"I just did what I did," he whispered in response, receiving a solid slap on the back.

"Then you just have to keep doing that, don't you?" Takumu laughed. "You still got our sights set on a lot of stuff, yeah? You just have to keep your eyes on those goals off in the far distance and fly without getting distracted. If you do that, I—all of us, will come chasing after you. Forever."

"Makes my back itchy when you say that...But it's true we don't have time for standing still. First, we have to give it our all in the Oscillatory fight today." Haruyuki gently touched the place on his left hand where the level-up bonus he had just obtained would be equipped.

No matter how large the Legion got, the fact that Kuroyuki-hime was its center would never change. Just like the first fixed star emitting an enormous gravitational pull in the center of a dark nebula.

The elevator arrived, and all twelve piled in, albeit like sardines in a can, and descended to the ground floor. The Saturday afternoon shopping mall was quite busy, but it seemed that their group with its mix of ages and uniforms was drawing attention nonetheless. But the squad of girls seemed to pay this absolutely no mind and proudly cut across the galleria with the two boys in tow at the end until they came to a stop in a corner of the entrance hall.

In the front garden that opened up outside the main building, the redbrick paths shone, pale in the midsummer sun. Beyond this light, the merger meeting that would determine the future of the Legion awaited—and the battle with Oscillatory Universe.

Kuroyukihime spun around, her black hair swinging gently.

Standing in the powerful sunlight, her outline shone hazily, almost as though she were wrapped in an aura of light. The Legion Master looked at each of the party in turn and made her crisp voice ring out.

"Now…let's go!"

**To be continued.**

# AFTERWORD

Thank you so much for reading *Accel World 19: Pull of the Dark Nebula*. Although, when I wrote that, I thought *Wait. Is it really the nineteenth book? It's not, like, number seventeen?* I had to check, but it is indeed Volume 19. Aah, in the blink of an eye, there are so many volumes…

I started the current arcs of Big Sister and White King in Volume 17, so this means those are already on their third book. Finally, all the bits and pieces have been put in place, so it's at last time for the big battle. I do hope I can bring that fight to a conclusion in the next volume somehow. (From here on, I will be touching on some details from the novel, so please do be aware!)

In this nineteenth volume, the situation with Nega Nebulus changes significantly. Initially, I thought the number of Legion members would increase steadily after Fuko and the rest of the Four Elements joined, but for some reason, everyone all joined at once in this volume. Takumu himself said it in the book, but the imbalance in the ratio of boys and girls in the Legion is at last starting to feel dangerous, so I'd like to get some balance there going forward. Although I don't get the sense that that will be easy. (LOL.)

To start with, if the merger with the neighboring Legion happens, then the number of M-types on the roll should increase a fair bit. At any rate, on the cover, too, we finally have seen the other members of the Triplex, Cassi and Pokki. I think they'll be powerful allies, so I do hope you'll be rooting for them!

Now, then. I believe this will also be announced in the Dengeki Bunko Fall 2015 Fair ahead of the release of this Volume 19, but they're going to make a new anime of *Accel World*! Production will, of course, be done by Sunrise Studio No. 8, and the main personnel will be coming on board from the TV anime. I'm deeply grateful to all of them, as well as everyone who expended every effort to make this project happen, and of course, all the readers who have been cheering for *Accel World* all this time.

I believe the details will be announced in all mediums going forward, but time-wise, the story will be a little in the future from the current White Legion arc. In advance of the package release, there will also be a theatrical release, so I'd be delighted if you could enjoy it on the big screen.

I must once again thank illustrator HIMA, who continues to draw the most impressive spreads of the squad of girl characters who continue to grow in number, and my editor, Miki, who manages the tightrope schedule with deft beauty. All right, everyone, I'll see you again in Volume 20!

Reki Kawahara
A day in September 2015

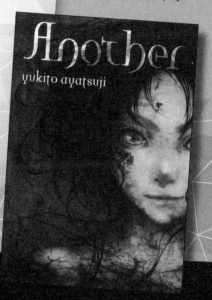

ACCEL WORLD, Volume 19
REKI KAWAHARA

Translation by Jocelyne Allen
Cover art by HIMA

ACCEL WORLD Vol. 19
© REKI KAWAHARA 2015
First published in Japan in 2015 by KADOKAWA CORPORATION,
Tokyo.
English translation rights arranged with KADOKAWA CORPORA-
TION, Tokyo, through Tuttle-Mori Agency, Inc., Tokyo.

English translation © 2019 by Yen Press, LLC

Yen On
150 West 30th Street, 19th Floor
New York, NY 10001

Visit us at yenpress.com
facebook.com/yenpress
twitter.com/yenpress
yenpress.tumblr.com
instagram.com/yenpress

First Yen On Edition: September 2019

Yen On is an imprint of Yen Press, LLC.
The Yen On name and logo are trademarks of Yen Press, LLC.

Library of Congress Cataloging-in-Publication Data
Names: Kawahara, Reki, author. | HIMA (Comic book artist) illustrator. |
    bee-pee, designer. | Allen, Jocelyne, 1974- translator.
Title: Accel World / Reki Kawahara ; illustrations, HIMA ; design, bee-pee ;
    translation by Jocelyne Allen.
Description: First Yen On edition. | New York, NY : Yen On, 2014–
Identifiers: LCCN 2014025099 | ISBN 9780316376730 (v. 1 : pbk.) |
    ISBN 9780316296366 (v. 2 : pbk.) | ISBN 9780316296373 (v. 3 : pbk.) |
    ISBN 9780316296380 (v. 4 : pbk.) | ISBN 9780316296397 (v. 5 : pbk.) |
    ISBN 9780316296403 (v. 6 : pbk.) | ISBN 9780316358194 (v. 7 : pbk.) |
    ISBN 9780316317610 (v. 8 : pbk.) | ISBN 9780316502702 (v. 9 : pbk.) |
    ISBN 9780316466059 (v. 10 : pbk.) | ISBN 9780316466066 (v. 11 : pbk.) |
    ISBN 9780316466073 (v. 12 : pbk.) | ISBN 9781975300067 (v. 13 : pbk.) |
    ISBN 9781975327231 (v. 14 : pbk.) | ISBN 9781975327255 (v. 15 : pbk.) |
    ISBN 9781975327279 (v. 16 : pbk.) | ISBN 9781975327293 (v. 17 : pbk.) |
    ISBN 9781975327316 (v. 18 : pbk.) | ISBN 9781975332181 (v. 19 : pbk.)
Subjects: CYAC: Science fiction. | Virtual reality—Fiction. | Fantasy.
Classification: LCC PZ7.K1755Kaw 2014 | DDC [Fic]—dc23
LC record available at https://lccn.loc.gov/2014025099

ISBNs: 978-1-9753-3218-1 (paperback)
       978-1-9753-3270-9 (ebook)

10 9 8 7 6 5 4 3 2 1

LSC-C

Printed in the United States of America